The Road to the Shore

and other stories

MICHAEL McLAVERTY

poolbeg press

This collection first published 1976 by
Poolbeg Press Ltd.,
Knocksedan House,
Swords, Co. Dublin, Ireland.

This edition 1982.

The generous assistance of the Arts Council of Northern Ireland and An Chomhairle Ealaion: The Arts Council in the publication of this book is gratefully acknowledged.

Cover by Robert Ballagh.
Designed by Steven Hope.

Printed by Cahill Printers Limited,
East Wall Road, Dublin 3.

Contents

Some of the stories in this collection were chosen from *The Game Cock*. Others have previously appeared only in periodicals, and acknowledgements are due to the editors of *The Dublin Magazine, Kilkenny Magazine, Threshold, The Capuchin Annual,* and *The Irish Press* 'New Irish Writing', in whose pages they were first published.

For Robert Greacen,
Roy McFadden and
John Boyd

The Road to the Shore

''Tis going to be a lovely day, thanks be to God,' sighed Sister Paul to herself, as she rubbed her wrinkled hands together and looked out at the thrushes hopping across the lawn. 'And it was a lovely day last year and the year before,' she mused, and in her mind saw the fresh face of the sea where, in an hour or two, she and the rest of the community would be enjoying their annual trip to the shore. 'And God knows it may be my last trip,' she said resignedly, and gazed abstractedly at a butterfly that was purring its wings against the sunny pane. She opened the window and watched the butterfly swing out into the sweet air, zigzagging down to a cushion of flowers that bordered the lawn. 'Isn't it well Sister Clare wasn't here,' she said to herself, 'for she'd be pestering the very soul out of me with her questions about butterflies and birds and flowers and the fall of dew?' She gave her girdle of beads a slight rattle. Wasn't it lovely to think of the pleasure that little butterfly would have when it found the free air under its wings again and its little feet pressing on the soft petals of the flowers and not on the hard pane? She always maintained it was better to enjoy Nature without searching and probing and chattering about the what and the where and the wherefore. But Sister Clare!—what she got out of it all, goodness only knew, for she'd give nobody a minute's peace—not a moment's peace would she give to a saint, living or dead. 'How long would that butterfly live in the air of a classroom?' she'd be asking. 'Do you think it would use up much of the active part of the air—the oxygen part, I mean? . . . What family would that butterfly belong to? . . . You know it's wrong to say that a butterfly lives only a day . . . When I am teaching my little pupils I always try to be accurate. I don't believe in stuffing their heads with fantastical nonsense however pleasurable it may be . . . ' Sister Paul turned round as if someone had suddenly walked into the room, and she was relieved when she saw nothing only the quiet vacancy of the room, the varnished desks with the sun on them and their reflections on the parquet floor.

She hoped she wouldn't be sitting beside Clare in the car today! She'd have no peace with her—not a bit of peace to look out at the countryside and see what changes had taken place inside twelve months. But Reverend Mother, she knew, would arrange all that—and if it'd be her misfortune to be parked beside Clare she'd have to accept it with resignation; yes, with resignation, and in that case her journey to the sea would be like a pilgrimage.

At that moment a large limousine drove up the gravel path, and as it swung round to the convent door she saw the flowers flow across its polished sides in a blur of colour. She hurried out of the room and down the stairs. In the hall Sister Clare and Sister Benignus were standing beside two baskets and Reverend Mother was staring at the stairs. 'Where were you, Sister Paul?' she said with mild reproof. 'We searched the whole building for you . . . We're all ready this ages . . . And Sister Francis has gone to put out the cat. Do you remember last year it had been in all the time we were at the shore and it ate the bacon?' As she spoke a door closed at the end of the corridor and Sister Francis came along, polishing her specs with the corner of her veil. Reverend Mother glanced away from her, that continual polishing of the spectacles irritated her; and then that empty expression on Sister Francis's face when the spectacles were off—vacuous, that's what it was!

'All ready now,' Reverend Mother tried to say without any trace of perturbation. Sister Clare and Sister Benignus lifted two baskets at their feet, Reverend Mother opened the hall-door, and they all glided out into the flat sunlight.

The doors of the car were wide open, the engine purring gently, and a perfume of new leather fingering the air. The chauffeur, a young man, touched his cap and stood deferentially to the side. Reverend Mother surveyed him quickly, noting his clean-bright face and white collar. 'I think there'll be room for us all in the back,' she said.

'There's a seat in the front, Sister,' the young man said, touching his cap again.

'Just put the baskets on it, if you please,' said Reverend Mother. And Sister Clare who, at that moment, was smiling at her own grotesque reflection in the back of the car came forward with her basket, Sister Benignus following. Sister Paul sighed audibly and fingered her girdle of beads.

'Now, Sister Paul, you take one of the corner seats, Sister Clare you sit beside her, and Sister Benignus and Sister Francis on the spring-up seats facing them—they were just made for you, the tiny tots!' And they all laughed, a brittle laugh that emphasized the loveliness of the day.

When they were all seated, Reverend Mother made sure that the hall-door was locked, glanced at the fastened windows, and then stood for a minute watching the gardener who was pushing his lawn-mower with unusual vigour and concentration. He stopped abruptly when her shadow fell across his path. 'And, Jack,' she said, as if continuing a conversation that had been interrupted, 'you'll have that lawn finished today?'

'Yes, Mother,' and he took off his hat and held it in

front of his breast. 'To be sure I'll have it finished today. Sure what'd prevent me to finish it, and this the grandest day God sent this many a long month—a wholesome day!'

'And, Jack, I noticed some pebbles on the lawn yesterday—white ones.'

'I remarked them myself, Mother. A strange terrier disporting himself in the garden done it.'

'Did it!'

'Yes, Mother, he did it with his two front paws, scratching at the edge of the lawn like it was a rabbit burrow. He done it yesterday, and when I clodded him off the grounds he'd the impertinence to go out a different way than he came in. But I've now his entrances and exits all blocked and barricaded and I'm afraid he'll have to find some other constituency to disport himself. Dogs is a holy terror for bad habits.'

'Be sure and finish it all today,' she said with some impatience. She turned to go away, hesitated, and turned back. 'By the way, Jack, if there are any drips of oil made by the car on the gravel you'll scuffle fresh pebbles over them.'

'I'll do that. But you need have no fear of oil from her engine,' and he glanced over at the limousine. 'She'll be as clean as a Swiss clock. 'Tis them grocery vans that leak--top, tail and middle.'

Crossing to the car, she heard with a feeling of pleasure the surge of the lawn-mower over the grass. Presently the car swung out of the gate on to a tree-lined road at the edge of the town. The nuns relaxed, settled themselves more comfortably in their seats and chatted about the groups on bicycles that were all heading for the shore.

'We will go to the same quiet strip as last year,' said Reverend Mother, and then as she glanced out of the window a villa on top of a hill drew her attention. 'There's a house that has been built since last year,' she said.

'No, no,' said Sister Francis. 'It's more than a year old for I remember seeing it last year,' and she peered at it through her spectacles.

Reverend Mother spoke through the speaking-tube to the driver: 'Is that villa on the hill newly built?' she asked.

He stopped the car. 'A doctor by the name of McGrath built it two years ago,' he said. 'He's married to a daughter of Solicitor O'Kane.'

'Oh, thank you,' said Reverend Mother; and the car proceeded slowly up the long hill above the town.

Sister Francis took of her spectacles, blew her breath on them, and rubbed them with her handkerchief. She took another look at the villa and said with obvious pride: 'A fine site, indeed. I remember last year that they had that little gadget over the door.'

'The architrave,' said Sister Clare importantly.

'Aye,' said Sister Paul, and she looked out at the trees and below them the black river with its strings of froth moving through the valley. How lovely it would be, she thought, to sit on the edge of that river, dabble her parched feet in it and send bubbles out into the race of the current. She had often done that when she was a child, and now that river and its trees, which she only saw once a year, brought her childhood back to her. She sighed and opened the window so as to hear the mumble of the river far below them. The breeze whorled in, and as it lifted their veils they all smiled, invigorated by the fresh loveliness of the air. A bumble bee flew in and crawled up the pane at Reverend Mother's side of the car. She opened the window and assisted the bee towards the opening with the top of her fountain-pen, but the bee clung to the pen and as she tried to shake it free the wind carried it in again. 'Like everything else it hates to leave you,' said Sister Benignus. Reverend Mother smiled and the bee flew up to the roof of the car and then alighted on the window beside Sister Paul. Sister Paul swept the bee to safety with the back of her hand.

'You weren't one bit afraid of it,' said Sister Clare. 'And if it had stung you, you would in a way have been responsible for its death. If it had been a Queen bee—though Queens wouldn't be flying at this time of the year—you would have been responsible for the deaths of potential thousands. A Queen bumble bee lays over two thousand eggs in one season!'

'Tis a great pity we haven't a hen like that,' put in Sister Francis, and they all laughed except Sister Clare. Sister Francis laughted till her eyes watered and, once more, she took off her spectacles. Reverend Mother fidgeted slightly and, in order to control her annoyance, she fixed her gaze on Sister Clare and asked her to continue her interesting account of the life of bumble bees. Sister Paul put her hands in her sleeves and sought distraction in the combings of cloud that streaked the sky.

Reverend Mother pressed her toe on the floor of the car and, instead of listening to Sister Clare, she was glaring unconsciously at Sister Francis who was tapping her spectacles on the palm of her hand and giving an odd laugh.

'Your spectacles are giving you much trouble today,' she broke in, unable any longer to restrain herself. 'Perhaps you would like to sit in the middle. It may provide your poor eyes with some rest.'

'No, thank you,' said Sister Francis, 'I like watching the crowds of cyclists passing on the road. But sometimes the sun glints on their handlebars and blinds me for a moment and makes me feel that a tiny thread or two has congregated on my lenses. It's my imagination of course.'

'Maybe you would care to have a look at *St. Anthony's Annals,*' and Reverend Mother handed her the magazine.

'Thank you, Mother. I'll keep it until we reach the

shore, for the doctor told me not to read in moving vehicles.'

The car rolled on slowly and when it reached the top of a hill, where there was a long descent of five miles to the sea, a strange silence came over the nuns, and each became absorbed in her own premeditation on the advancing day. 'Go slowly down the hill,' Reverend Mother ordered the driver.

Boys sailed past them on bicycles, and when some did so with their hands off the handlebars a little cry of amazement would break from Sister Francis and she would discuss with Sister Clare the reckless irresponsibility of boys and the worry they must bring to their parents.

Suddenly at a bend on the hill they all looked at Sister Paul for she was excitedly drawing their attention to a line of young poplars. 'Look, look!' she was saying. 'Look at the way their leaves are dancing and not a flicker out of the other trees. And to think I never noticed them before!'

'I think they are aspens,' said Sister Clare, 'and anyway they are not indigenous to this country.'

'We had four poplars in our garden when I was growing up—black poplars, my father called them,' said Sister Paul, lost in her own memory.

'What family did they belong to? There's *angustifolia, laurifolia,* and *balsamifera* and others among the poplar family.'

'I don't know what family they belonged to,' Sister Paul went on quietly. 'I only know they were beautiful —beautiful in very early spring when every tree and twig around them would still be bleak—and there they were bursting into leaf, a brilliant yellow leaf like a flake of sunshine. My father, God be good to his kindly soul, planted four of them when I was young, for there were four in our family, all girls, and one of the trees my father called Kathleen, another Teresa, another Eileen, and lastly my own, Maura. And I remember how he used to stand at the dining-room window gazing out at the young poplars with the frost white and hard around them. "I see a leaf or two coming on Maura," he used to say, and we would all rush to the window and gaze into the garden, each of us fastening her eye on her own tree and then measuring its growth of leaf with the others. And to the one whose tree was first in leaf he used to give a book or a pair of rosary beads . . . Poor Father,' she sighed, and fumbled in her sleeve for her handkerchief.

'Can you not think of what special name those trees had?' pressed Clare. 'Did their leaves tremble furiously —*tremula, tremuloides*?'

'They didn't quiver very much,' said Sister Paul, her head bowed. 'My father didn't plant aspens, I remember. He told us it was from an aspen that Our Saviour's rood was made, and because their leaves remember the Crucifixion they are always trembling . . . But our poplars had a lovely warm perfume when they were leafing and that perfume always reminded my father of autumn. Wasn't that strange?' she addressed the whole car, 'a tree coming into leaf and it reminding my poor father of autumn.'

'I know its family now,' said Clare, clapping her hands together. '*Balsamifera*—that's the family it belonged to—it's a native of Northern Italy.'

'And I remember,' said Paul, folding and unfolding her handkerchief on her lap, 'how my poor father had no gum once to wrap up a newspaper that he was posting. It was in winter and he went out to the poplars and dabbed his finger here and there on the sticky buds and smeared it on the edge of the wrapping paper.'

'That was enough to kill the buds,' said Clare. 'The gum, as you call it, is their only protective against frost.'

'It was himself he killed,' said Paul. 'He had gone out

from a warm fire in his slippers, out into the bleak air and got his death.'

'And what happened to the poplars?' said Clare. But Sister Paul had turned her head to the window again and was trying to stifle the tears that were rising to her eyes.

'What other trees grew in your neighbourhood?' continued Clare. Sister Paul didn't seem to hear her, but when the question was repeated she turned and said slowly: 'I'm sorry that I don't know their names. But my father, Lord have mercy on him, used to say that a bird could leap from branch to branch for ten miles around without using its wings.'

Sister Clare smiled and Reverend Mother nudged her with her elbow, signing to her to keep quiet; and when she, herself, glanced at Paul she saw the sun shining through the fabric of her veil and a handkerchief held furtively to her eyes.

There was silence now in the sun-filled car while outside cyclists continued to pass them, free-wheeling down the long hill. Presently there was a rustle of paper in the car as Sister Francis drew forth from her deep pocket a bag of soft peppermints, stuck together by the heat. Carefully she peeled the bits of paper off the sweets, and as she held out the bag to Reverend Mother she said : 'Excuse my fingers.' But Reverend Mother shook her head, and Clare and Benignus, seeing that she had refused, felt it would be improper for them to accept. Francis shook the bag towards Paul but since she had her eyes closed, as if in prayer, she neither saw nor heard what was being offered to her. *'In somno pacis,'* said Francis, popping two peppermints into her own mouth and hiding the bag in her wide sleeve. 'A peppermint is soothing and cool on a hot day like this,' she added with apologetic good nature.

A hot smell of peppermint drifted around the car. Reverend Mother lowered her window to its full length, and though the air rushed in in soft folds around her face it was unable to quench the flaming odour. Somehow, for Reverend Mother, the day, that had hardly begun yet, was spoiled by an old nun with foolish habits and by a young nun unwise enough not to know when to stop questioning. Everything was going wrong, and it would not surprise her that before evening clouds of rain would blow in from the sea and blot out completely the soft loveliness of the sunny day. Once more she looked at Paul, and, seeing her head bowed in thought, she knew that there was some aspect of the countryside, some shape in cloud or bush, that brought back to Paul a sweet but sombre childhood. For herself she had no such memories—there was nothing in her own life, she thought, only a mechanical ordering, a following of routine, that may have brought some pleasure into other people's lives but none to her own. However, she'd do her best to make the day pleasant for them; after all, it was only one day in the year and if the eating of peppermints gave Sister Francis some satisfaction it was not right to thwart her.

She smiled sweetly then at Francis and as Francis offered the sweets once more, and she was stretching forward to take one there was a sudden dunt to the back of the car and a crash of something falling on the road. The car stopped and the nuns looked at one another, their heads bobbing in consternation. They saw the driver raise himself slowly from his seat, walk back the road, and return again with a touch of his cap at the window.

'A slight accident, Sister,' he said, addressing Reverend Mother. 'A cyclist crashed into our back wheel. But it's nothing serious, I think.'

Reverend Mother went out leaving the door open, and through it there came the free sunlight, the cool air, and the hum of people talking. She was back again in a few minutes with her handkerchief dabbed with blood, and collected other handkerchiefs from the nuns, who followed her out on to the road. Sister Paul stood back and saw amongst the bunch of people a young man reclining on the bank of the road, a hand to his head. 'I can't stand the sight of blood,' she said to herself, her fingers clutching her rosary beads. She beckoned to a lad who was resting on his bicycle : 'Is he badly hurt, lad? He'll not die, will he?'

'Not a bit of him, Sister. He had his coat folded over the handlebars and the sleeve of it caught in the wheel and flung him against the car.'

'Go up, like a decent boy, and have a good look at him again.'

But before the lad had reached the group the chauffeur had assisted the injured man to his feet and was leading him to the car. The handkerchiefs were tied like a turban about his head, his trousers were torn at the knee, and a holy medal was pinned to his braces.

'Put his coat on or he'll catch cold,' Reverend Mother was saying.

'Och, Sister, don't worry about me,' the man was saying. 'Sure it was my own fault. Ye weren't to blame at all. I'll go back again on my own bicycle—I'm fit enough.'

Reverend Mother consulted the chauffeur and whatever advice he gave her the injured man was put into the back of the car. Sister Francis was ordered into the vacant seat beside the driver, the baskets were handed to Paul and Clare, and when the man's bicycle was tied to the carrier they drove off for the hospital in the town.

The young man, sitting between Reverend Mother and Sister Paul, shut his eyes in embarrassment, and when the blood oozed through the pile of handkerchiefs Reverend Mother took the serviettes from the baskets and tied them round his head and under his chin, and all the time the man kept repeating : 'I'm a sore trouble to you, indeed. And sure it was my own fault.' She told him to button his coat or he would catch cold, and when he had done so she noticed a Total Abstinence badge in the lapel.

'A good clean-living man,' she thought, and to think that he was the one to meet with an injury while many an old drunkard could travel the roads of Ireland on a bicycle and arrive home without pain or scratch or cough.

'Tis a blessing of God you weren't killed,' she said, with a rush of protectiveness, and she reached for the thermos flask from the basket and handed the man a cup of tea.

Now and again Sister Paul would steal a glance at him, but the sight of his pale face and the cup trembling in his hand and rattling on the saucer made her turn to the window where she tried to lose herself in contemplation. But all her previous mood was now scattered from her mind, and she could think of nothing only the greatness of Reverend Mother and the cool way she took command of an incident that would have left the rest of them weak and confused.

'How are you feeling now?' she could hear Reverend Mother asking. 'Would you like another sandwich?'

'No, thank you, Sister; sure I had my good breakfast in me before I left the house. I'm a labouring man and since I'm out of work this past three months my wife told me to go off on the bike and have a swim with myself. I was going to take one of the youngsters on the bar of the bike but my wife wouldn't let me.'

'She had God's grace about her,' said Reverend Mother. 'That should be a lesson to you,' and as she refilled his cup from the thermos flask she thought that if the young man had been killed they, in a way, would have had to provide his widow and children with some help. 'And we were only travelling slowly,' she found herself saying aloud.

'Sure, Sister, no one knows that better than myself. You were keeping well in to your own side of the road and when I was ready to sail past you on the hill my coat caught in the front wheel and my head hit the back of your car.'

'S-s-s,' and the nuns drew in their breath with shrinking solicitude.

They drove up to the hospital, and after Reverend Mother had consulted the doctor and was told that the wound was only a slight abrasion and contusion she returned light-heartedly to the car. Sister Clare made no remark when she heard the news but as the wheels of the car rose and fell on the road they seemed to echo what was in her mind : *abrasion and contusion, abrasion and contusion.* 'Abrasion and contusion of what?' she asked herself. 'Surely the doctor wouldn't say "head"—abrasion and contusion of the head?' No, there must be some medical term that Reverend Mother had withheld from them, and as she was about to probe Reverend Mother for the answer the car swung unexpectedly into the convent avenue. 'Oh,' she said with disappointment, and when alighting from the car and seeing Sister Francis give the remains of her sweets to the chauffeur she knew that for her, too, the day was at an end.

They all passed inside except Reverend Mother who stood on the steps at the door noting the quiet silence of the grounds and the heat-shadows flickering above the flower-beds. With a mocking smile she saw the lawn-mower at rest on the uncut lawn and found herself mimicking the gardener : 'I'll have it all finished today, Sister, I'll have it all finished today.' She put a hand to her throbbing head and crossed the gravel path to look for him, and there in the clump of laurel bushes she found him fast asleep, his hat over his face to keep off the flies, and three empty porter bottles beside him. She tiptoed away from him. 'He has had a better day than we have had,' she said to herself, 'so let him sleep it out, for it's the last he'll have at my expense . . . Oh, drink is a curse,' and she thought of the injury that had befallen the young man with the Abstinence Badge and he as sober as any judge. Then she drew up suddenly as something quick and urgent came into her mind : 'Of course!—he would take the job as gardener, and he unemployed this past three months!' With head erect she sped quickly across the grass and into the convent. Sister Paul was still in the corridor when she saw Reverend Mother lift the phone and ring up the hospital : 'Is he still there? . . . He's all right? . . . That's good . . . Would you tell him to call to see me sometime this afternoon?' There was a transfigured look on her face as she put down the receiver and strode across to Sister Paul. 'Sister Paul,' she said, 'you may tell the other Sisters that on tomorrow we will set out again for the shore.' Sister Paul smiled and whisked away down the corridor : 'Isn't Reverend Mother great the way she can handle things?' she said to herself. 'And to think that on tomorrow I'll be able to see the poplars again.'

The Poteen Maker

When he taught me some years ago he was an old man near his retirement, and when he would pass through the streets of the little town on his way from school you would hear the women talking about him as they stood at their doors knitting or nursing their babies : 'Poor man, he's done . . . Killing himself . . . Digging his own grave!' With my bag of books under my arm I could hear them, but I could never understand why they said he was digging his own grave, and when I would ask my mother she would scold me : 'Take your dinner, like a good boy, and don't be listening to the hard backbiters of this town. Your father has always a good word for Master Craig—so that should be enough for you!'

'But why do they say he's killing himself?'

'Why do who say? Didn't I tell you to take your dinner and not be repeating what the idle gossips of this town are saying? Listen to me, son! Master Craig is a decent, good-living man—a kindly man that would go out of his way to do you a good turn. If Master Craig was in any other town he'd have got a place in the new school at the Square instead of being stuck for ever in that wee poky bit of a school at the edge of the town!'

It was true that the school was small—a two-roomed ramshackle of a place that lay at the edge of the town beyond the last street lamp. We all loved it. Around it grew a few trees, their trunks hacked with boys' names and pierced with nibs and rusty drawing-pins. In summer when the windows were open we could hear the leaves rubbing together and in winter see the raindrops hanging on the bare twigs.

It was a draughty place and the master was always complaining of the cold, and even in the early autumn he would wear his overcoat in the classroom and rub his hands together : 'Boys, it's very cold today. Do you feel it cold?' And to please him we would answer : 'Yes, sir, 'tis very cold.' He would continue to rub his hands and he would look out at the old trees casting their leaves or at the broken spout that flung its tail of rain against the window. He always kept his hands clean and three times a day he would wash them in a basin and wipe them on a roller towel affixed to the inside of his press. He had a hanger for his coat and a brush to brush away the chalk that accumulated on the collar in the course of the day.

In the wet, windy month of November three buckets were placed on the top of the desks to catch the drips that plopped here and there from the ceiling, and those drops made different music according to the direction of the wind. When the buckets were filled the master always called me to empty them, and I would take them one at a time and swirl them into the drain at the street and stand for a minute gazing down at the wet roofs of the town or listen to the rain pecking at the lunch-papers scattered about on the cinders.

'What's it like outside?' he always asked when I came in with the empty buckets.

'Sir, 'tis very bad.'

He would write sums on the board and tell me to keep an eye on the class, and out to the porch he would go and stand in grim silence watching the rain nibbling at the puddles. Sometimes he would come in and I would see him sneak his hat from the press and disappear for five or ten minutes. We would fight then with rulers or paper-darts till our noise would disturb the mistress next door and in she would come and stand with her lips compressed, her finger in her book. There was silence as she upbraided us : 'Mean, low, good-for-nothing corner boys. Wait'll Mister Craig comes back and I'll let him know the angels he has. And I'll give him special news about *you*!'—and she shakes her book at me : 'An altar boy on Sunday and a corner boy for the rest of the week!' We would let her barge away, the buckets plink-plonking as they filled up with rain and her own class beginning to hum, now that she was away from them.

When Mr. Craig came back he would look at us and ask if we disturbed Miss Lagan. Our silence or our tossed hair always gave him the answer. He would correct the sums on the board, flivell the pages of a book with his thumb, and listen to us reading; and occasionally he would glance out of the side-window at the river that flowed through the town and, above it, the bedraggled row of houses whose tumbling yard-walls sheered to the water's edge. 'The loveliest county in Ireland is County Down!' he used to say, with a sweep of his arm to the river and the tin cans and the chalked walls of the houses.

During that December he was ill for two weeks and when he came back amongst us he was greatly failed. To keep out the draughts he nailed perforated plywood over the ventilators and stuffed blotting paper between the wide crevices at the jambs of the door. There were muddy marks of a ball on one of the windows and on one pane a long crack with fangs at the end of it : 'So someone has drawn the River Ganges while I was away,' he said; and whenever he came to the geography of India he would refer to the Ganges delta by pointing to the cracks on the pane.

When our ration of coal for the fire was used up he would send me into the town with a bucket, a coat over my head to keep off the rain, and the money in my fist to buy a stone of coal. He always gave me a penny to buy sweets for myself, and I can always remember that he kept his money in a waistcoat pocket. Back again I would come with the coal and he would give me disused exercise books to light the fire. 'Chief stoker!' he called me, and the name has stuck to me to this day.

It was at this time that the first snow had fallen, and someone by using empty potato bags had climbed over the glass-topped wall and stolen the school coal, and for some reason Mr. Craig did not send me with the bucket to buy more. The floor was continually wet from our boots, and our breaths frosted the windows. Whenever the door opened a cold draught would rush in and gulp down the breath-warmed air in the room. We would jig our feet and sit on our hands to warm them. Every half-hour Mr. Craig would make us stand and while he lilted *O'Donnell Abu* we did a series of physical exercises which he had taught us, and in the excitement and the exaltation we forgot about our sponging boots and the snow that pelted against the windows. It was then that he did his lessons on Science; and we were delighted to see the bunsen burner attached to the gas bracket which hung like an inverted T from the middle of the ceiling. The snoring bunsen seemed to heat up the room and we all gathered round it, pressing in on top of it till he scattered us back to our places with the cane : 'Sit down!' he would shout. 'There's no call to stand. Everybody will be able to see!'

The cold spell remained, and over and over again he repeated one lesson in Science, which he called : *Evaporation and Condensation.*

'I'll show you how to purify the dirtiest of water,' he had told us. 'Even the filthiest water from the old river could be made fit for drinking purposes.' In a glass trough he had a dark brown liquid and when I got his back turned I dipped my finger in it and it tasted like treacle or burnt candy, and then I remembered about packets of brown sugar and tins of treacle I had seen in his press.

He placed some of the brown liquid in a glass retort and held it aloft to the class : 'In the retort I have water which I have discoloured and made impure. In a few minutes I'll produce from it the clearest of spring water.' And his weary eyes twinkled, and although we could see nothing funny in that, we smiled because he smiled.

The glass retort was set up with the flaming bunsen underneath, and as the liquid was boiling, the steam was trapped in a long-necked flask on which I sponged cold water. With our eyes we followed the bubbling mixture and the steam turning into drops and dripping rapidly into the flask. The air was filled with a biscuity smell, and the only sound was the snore of the bunsen. Outside was the cold air and the falling snow. Presently the master turned out the gas and held up the flask containing the clear water.

'As pure as crystal!' he said, and we watched him pour some of it into a tumbler, hold it in his delicate fingers, and put it to his lips. With wonder we watched him drink it and then our eyes travelled to the dirty, cakey scum that had congealed on the glass sides of the retort. He pointed at this with his ruler : 'The impurities are sifted out and the purest of pure water remains.' And for some reason he gave his roguish smile. He filled up the retort again with the dirty brown liquid and repeated the experiment until he had a large bottle filled with the purest of pure water.

The following day it was still snowing and very cold. The master filled up the retort with the clear liquid which he had stored in the bottle : 'I'll boil this again to show you that there are no impurities left.' So once again we watched the water bubbling, turning to steam, and then to shining drops. Mr. Craig filled up his tumbler : 'As pure as crystal,' he said, and then the door opened and in walked the Inspector. He was muffled to the ears and snow covered his hat and his attaché case. We all stared at him—he was the old, kind man whom we had seen before. He glanced at the bare firegrate and at the closed windows with their sashes edged with snow. The water continued to bubble in the retort, giving out its pleasant smell.

The Inspector shook hands with Mr. Craig and they talked and smiled together, the Inspector now and again looking towards the empty grate and shaking his head. He unrolled his scarf and flicked the snow from off his shoulders and from his attaché case. He sniffed the air, rubbed his frozen hands together, and took a black notebook from his case. The snow ploofed against the windows, the wind hummed under the door.

'Now, boys,' Mr. Craig continued, holding up the tumbler of water from which a thread of steam wriggled in the air. He talked to us in a strange voice and told us about the experiment as if we were seeing it for the first time. Then the Inspector took the warm tumbler and questioned us on our lesson. 'It should be perfectly pure water,' he said, and he sipped at it. He tasted its flavour. He sipped at it again. He turned to Mr. Craig. They whispered together, the Inspector looking towards the retort which was still bubbling and sending out its twirls of steam to be condensed to water of purest crystal. He laughed loudly, and we smiled when he again put the tumbler to his lips and this time drank it all. Then he asked us more questions and told us how, if we were shipwrecked, we could make pure water from the salt sea water.

Mr. Craig turned off the bunsen and the Inspector spoke to him. The master filled up the Inspector's tumbler and poured out some for himself in a cup. Then the Inspector made jokes with us, listened to us singing, and told us we were the best class in Ireland. Then he gave us a few sums to do in our books. He put his hands in his pockets and jingled his money, rubbed a little peep-hole in the breath-covered window and peered out at the loveliest sight in Ireland. He spoke to Mr. Craig again and Mr. Craig shook hands with him and they both laughed. The Inspector looked at his watch. Our class was let out early, and while I remained behind to tidy up the Science apparatus the master gave me an empty treacle tin to thrown in the bin and told me to carry the Inspector's case up to the station. I remember that day well as I walked behind them through the snow, carrying the attaché case, and how loudly they talked and laughed as the snow whirled cold from the river. I remember how they crouched together to light their cigarettes, how match after match was thrown on the road, and how they walked off with the unlighted cigarettes still in their mouths. At the station Mr. Craig took a penny from his waistcoat pocket and as he handed it to me it dropped on the snow. I lifted it and he told me I was the best boy in Ireland. . . .

When I was coming from his funeral last week—God have mercy on him—I recalled that wintry day and the feel of the cold penny and how much more I know now about Mr. Craig than I did then. On my way out of the town—I don't live there now—I passed the school and saw a patch of new slates on the roof and an ugly iron barrier near the door to keep the home-going children from rushing headlong on to the road. I knew if I had looked at the trees I'd have seen rusty drawing-pins stuck into their rough flesh. But I passed by. I heard there was a young teacher in the school now, with an array of coloured pencils in his breast pocket.

Uprooted

In the large flat field that lay between the sea-road and the farm-house the O'Briens were at the spring sowing, wasting no minute of the lovely spell of weather that had at last driven out the winter's cold from the soil. Jim, the married son, worked the horses and the plough, and his young wife dropped the potato seed on the manure that the old father was forking into the furrows. Two little boys, bread crumbs on their jerseys and jam on their cheeks, were occasionally carrying boxes of seed to their mother or pausing to watch their granda and telling him they wouldn't eat potatoes that grew on such smelly stuff.

'Ah, me boys, you'll be glad to eat anything if this accursed war lasts much longer,' he said to them, stuck his fork in the manure and took out his pipe. He blew through the shank and told the boys not to be lazy and to go and help their mother.

It was a fine April day, the sky a thin blue, larks loosening their throats in it, and a clean wind sweeping freely in from the sea and flattening the smoke from the fires of weeds and twigs that were burning in many of the fields around.

'There's great heart in that soil, Jim,' the old man called out as the son passed up field with the plodding horses.

'Ach, father, if there was some heart in the horses we'd have the field finished long ago.'

'They'll do us rightly till the war is over and then we'll get the tractor. We'll get it, son, never fear. Our name is down for one, high up in the list,' and he smiled as he watched the good-natured soil curve like brown water from the shining blades of the plough. 'They're pulling fine, Jim, and this weather will hold up.'

'If we'd the tractor we wouldn't worry what kind of weather it was. McKeever has three fields done and here we are plodding away with a pair of old horses.'

'Don't condemn the horses till she's delivered. Next spring, please God, the war will be over and we'll have the tractor.

'McKeever knew to get one before the war started,' the son said, urging on the horses. 'We're always late!'

'We'll drive her when she comes—won't we, granda?' one of the little boys said.

'You will, my lads, indeed you will. In a short while you'll be big lumps of fellas and you'll be able to give your granda a long rest,' and he spat on his hands and lifted the fork to do another spell of work.

'They are fine grandchildren, fine biddable boys,' he said to himself; 'and Jim had God's blessing about him when he married their mother. She's a good wife, a good daughter-in-law, a good worker—a whole trinity of goodness.' And he raised his head and looked across at her, bent over the drills, her wellingtons browned with clay, and her red head-scarf lifting in the wind. Beyond her was their comfortable farm-house and the baby's washing fluttering whitely on the clothes-line in the garden.

Everything looked lively, sheep calling to their lambs in the adjoining fields, gulls flying inland to the turned up soil, the twigs crackling in the fire at the foot of the field and the smoke taking the sting from the air. The sheepdog lay on an empty sack at the side of the hedge and the boys were piling the empty boxes at each side of him to make a kennel. Now and again they started in the direction of the fire, yearning to throw twigs on it. But they were forbidden to go near it, for yesterday some sparks had fallen on their jerseys and had burnt brown holes in them.

For devilment they threw pieces of sod at their granda when his back was turned, and when he looked towards their mother and not at them they began to laugh. They raised their heads and spied out the larks like crumbs of clay against the blue sky. They tried to count them but were forever losing sight of them or counting ones they had already counted before. Then a screeching of brakes made them turn their eyes to the sea-road where an army car with a canvas cover had pulled up.

'Soldiers!' the boys shouted.

'They'll shoot the pair of you', the granda called out as he saw them scamper to the foot of the field, the dog after them.

The granda rested his arms on the fork and saw five men, three in uniform, come out from the back of the jeep. They stretched their arms, stamped their feet on the road, and lit cigarettes. 'Nothing like the army for laziness,' he said to himself; 'if they'd wield this fork for an hour or two it'd slacken the hide on them.' The men gazed seawards, swung their arms back and forth to warm themselves and leisurely returned to the car and took things from the back of it. The old man spat out and eyed them with intense but puzzled curiosity. Two of the men paced the road, stretching a steel tape-measure that flashed in the sun like a live eel. They were up on the fence now, scanning the fields. The dog was barking at them, and the sheep in the nearby field were moving towards a grassy mound, the only hump to be seen in all that flat countryside.

The car moved some perches along the road and again the men got out, carrying with them a white pole with black and red markings.

Jim halted the horses when his father asked him what he thought the army men might be doing.

'God knows, father, what they're up to. They mightn't know themselves. Maybe they're going to plant a gun on top of the mound or make stores for bombs.'

'They'll plant no gun or no bombs on my land!'

They saw the strangers enter the sheep-field and close the gate behind them. They saw one place the white pole near the foot of the mound and another erect a gadget on a tripod, stoop and peer through it, his hands resting on his thighs.

'Divil's own cheek!' the old man said, and throwing down his fork he crossed the potato field and shouted across a narrow stream that divided it from the sheep-field.

'Eh, eh, what is it you're wanting there?'

'Surveying, old man, surveying!' one said and wrote something in a notebook he carried in his hand.

'Surveying what?'

They didn't answer him but lifted the tripod and marched off round the mound as if they knew the lie of the land as one reared on it.

All enthusiasm for his work drained away from the old man as he watched them disappear behind the small hill. He had heard of land being taken over by the armv in other parts of the county but had hoped that nothing like that would befall him. Not a square foot would he give them! Let them go and seize some boggy stretch that's no good for beast nor crop! He spat into the stream and buttoned his coat. He saw them come round from the back of the hill, saw them take the path past Dan Mullan's old house and heard Dan's old dog raise its hoarse bark. Horses had halted in other fields, and nothing moved now but gulls on the turned-up soil and the warm smoke from the fires drifting inland and hazing the distance.

In about two hours' time the strangers returned to the road and when their car had driven off the old man kept mumbling to himself, debating with his uneasy thoughts and urging Jim to quit for the day. He'd have no peace of mind till the meaning of this sudden trespass upon his land had been unravelled.

'Och, father, forget about them. We might never see light or sight of them again. They're probably some young officers learning about war.'

'And what kind of war could they learn about in an old field that grazes sheep? And why didn't they answer me civilly when I spoke to them? "Surveying" they said and walked off as if I was an old stump of a tree you'd strike a match on.'

'You needn't blame them. They're only carrying out orders.'

'I don't like it, Jim. They're up to no good. I don't like it I tell you!' and he struck the fork in the ground and told him to unyoke the horses.

And that evening he urged his son to hurry at his supper and cycle into the village to see if there was any talk about the strangers.

Old Dan Mullan came over for his usual visit. He knew nothing; the strangers had said nothing to him, didn't even bid him the time of day but marched on past his house with maps and strange-looking gear. No, they had no guns with them so far as he could see. Both agreed that it boded no good.

It was late that night when Jim came back and there was no one in the kitchen except the old man smoking at the fire and Mary smoothing the clothes at the table.

'There was talk and rumours of talk,' the son said as he hung up his cap at the back of the door.

'Aye.'

'No one knows for certain what's afoot. Some say they're going to build barracks of some sort.'

'But they can't build on a man's land without permission. Are all rights to be choked and smothered because there's a war on?'

'The government, they say, can do whatever they damn well like. They say they can seize a man's land and pay him compensation.'

'Nothing can compensate a man for the loss of his land!' the old man shouted and rose from his chair.

Mary looked towards the room where the children slept and the old man lowered his voice and told of the number of years the O'Briens had worked and tilled and improved that land outside. And do you think he was going to hand it over to any government to hack and ruin! He was not!

'No use, father, crossing a bridge before you come to it. There mightn't be a grain of truth in any of the rumours.'

'Sure if they were going to take over a field or two you'd be the first to hear of it, granda,' Mary said and brought him a light for his pipe that had gone out.

'I suppose you're right, Mary, I suppose you're right,' and he lifted a lamp and went out to have a look at the cows.

'Not a word to him, Mary,' Jim said in a low voice. 'But the sergeant in the village was saying he heard on good authority they were going to build an aerodrome in the flat of the land.'

II

During the next few days the car came again and the strange men in uniform were seen, crossing and recrossing neighbouring fields, and in the evenings they were gone leaving no traces behind them except the rib-marks of the car's tyres on the grassy side of the sea-road. And in the farmers' minds they left a disquieting curiosity that seized on every rumour and magnified it.

At the end of three weeks after showers of rain and the green potato tops struggling into vigorous life on the drills the postman handed a letter to Mary O'Brien.

'I've a fine handful of these letters with me this morning,' he said. 'I've even one for Dan Mullan.'

She looked at the letter, closed the door, and handed it to the old man. He opened it, saw the strange typescript, and gave it to his son to read. He read it slowly, and slower still came the realization of what it contained. They were ordered to leave their farm and have all goods and chattels thereon removed within three months. Compensation would be agreed upon by the parties concerned.

'I'm not going!' the old man shouted. 'I'm not stirring hand or foot from the land that reared me!' He strode about the kitchen, stamping his feet, and gazing out the window, his fists resting on the table.

'Sit down and take your breakfast, granda,' Mary said.

'I'll not eat till I come back. I'm going out.'

Jim and Mary stared at him, afraid to ask him where he was going. They saw him take his stick and go out along the sea-road, the dog at his heels.

The old man saw nothing, heard nothing, not even the plunge of the sea breaking on the stones below the road. He turned to the left, disappeared behind the grassy mound and headed for the priest's house. The priest had just finished his breakfast, the housekeeper clearing away the dishes when the old man rang the bell at the door. The housekeeper ushered him into the sittingroom where he sat, his eyes fixed on the chair-dents that were like paw-marks in the polished linoleum.

He gave the letter to the priest, and though the priest already knew what it would contain he read it slowly. A month ago he had already written a letter of protest about the prospective aerodrome and had pointed out that a grave-yard lay in the vicinity. His protest did not postpone the prepared plans and they assured him that the graveyard did not come within the boundaries of the commandeered territory.

'It's bad news, Tom,' he said folding the old man's letter. 'And it's hard news!'

'But surely, Father, they can't drive a man from his own land. Drive him out on the road like a pack of worthless tinkers.'

'They could drive me from mine if it stood in their way.'

The old man stared at him, uncomprehending, enraged at an unseen force against which priest nor man had any power.

'What's to be done, Father? We've no place to turn to. All our lives we've worked honestly, paid our debts, and buried our dead when their time came.'

The priest explained that there were others in the parish, all those in the hollow, who would get their notice to quit. He said something about the cruelty of war, about suffering, and about the cruel inhuman element that emerged from war's preparation and war's prolongation. He spoke of countries ravaged by war, countries where not one farmer or two farmers but thousands were driven out on the roads with nowhere to lay their heads. The old man listened, but everything the priest was saying seemed far away, like something out of a history book, something that bore no relation to him or his family.

'We can do nothing, Tom, but will what God wills,' and he rested his hand on the old man's shoulder. 'Make up your mind to go and get ready at once. And get a high valuation put on your land. That's my advice to you,' and he told him of the letter of protest he had written, and that there was no human feeling, no mercy, in officialdom.

'But maybe, Father, the war will end in three months.'

'It's not likely to end in three months—it may take years.'

'Then we'll have to go, Father. There's no hope anywhere.'

The priest nodded his head, aware of the foolishness of tethering the old man's mind to a hopeless hope.

'I'll bide by what you say. We'll go, but we'll try not to go far afield. A man of my years can't live far away from his own people. My people that lie at peace under the sod outside.'

'You have great courage, Tom, and God gives His grace to the courageous.'

The priest watched him go out, and from the window he watched him move among the mounds in the graveyard and kneel down, one hand resting on a headstone above the graves of his own people.

When he arrived home all fight had gone out of him as he sat at the table.

'Were you away to see about the tractor, granda?' one of his grandsons asked him.

'Tractor, son, what tractor?'

'Give your granda peace to take his breakfast. Run out and play yourselves like good boys.'

'Leave them alone, Mary, when the heart's cold the voice of a child can warm it,' and as he took his breakfast he told Jim to sell the sheep, then the cattle, but to leave the horses to the last.

A shower of rain fell, scoring the window pane with streaks of silver, and washing the dust from the potato leaves in the large flat field. There'd be a rich harvest there, but there'd be no one to harvest them, and in a short while no smoke would rise from the farmsteads and at night no comforting light shine out from Dan Mullan's across the wide fields. The larks would be free in the sky, but soon there wouldn't be the bark of a dog in the fields, and where children once played there would be nothing but huts peopled with strangers who had no wish to be there.

At night the old man went out alone with his dog, wandering the roads and calling in with Dan Mullan to shred his worries in useless talk. And then home again when the sky was a harvest of stars and the sea-waves breaking in unchanging sound upon the stones on the shore.

In June Dan Mullan went away. The O'Briens helped him to flit, his few sticks of furniture piled and roped on a cart, and Dan sitting on top of the old door. Easy for one man to leave and set up house again. Any old four walls that were still standing would do him. All he needed was to fling a few sheets of corrugated iron over them to keep out the rain. And that's what Dan did. He took possession of an old ruined house about two miles along the coast, patched the walls with cement, put down a new floor of concrete and had the two windows repaired. He placed his bed in a corner well away from the sparks of the fire and he often sat on it when old Tom called to see him.

'There's one blessing in it all,' he said to him one day, 'that they didn't order me out in the winter time. By the time the days harden this old place will be warmed up. It's not much of a place with the smell of rotten seaweed at your door—still it'll do me my days. And I've enough money from the old place that'll keep me out of debt.'

'The man who owns less is the best off.'

'Wherever you go, Tom, you'll always have the comfort of a family. A man can't have everything in this life and he must be content. Jim will find a good farm for you all with the compensation money.'

'Not with the war bringing high prices for sheep and cattle farmers are loth to sell their land. And I don't want to go far from here. You can't transplant an old bush. It'll wither in the richest soil.'

'In a short while you'll be coming back here to tell me of your good luck. You'll see that I'm right.'

But the O'Briens hadn't the luck Dan expected. There were no farms for sale and Jim didn't try hard to find one. His mind was set in starting a shop in Downpatrick, a town where his children would have schools at their own doorstep. But his chief difficulty was to coax his father into his way of thinking. And one evening when his father came in from Dan's Jim told him that the only farms to be had were in the county of Antrim.

'Antrim has cold, clabbery land—heavy land that'd kill them not used to it,' the father said. 'It's not like the dry loose soil of our own county. You may drop all notion of going there, Jim. Wherever we go it mustn't be far away from our own people.'

'What people, father?'

'Your own people that's at peace in the graveyard beyond.'

Jim paused, paused until he was sure that his memory and its associations had sunk below the present moment.

'What if we settled for a while in Downpatrick, father? It's only ten miles away.'

'You can't farm the streets of a town.'

'I was thinking we could start a shop there.'

'A shop!' and his father stared at him and spat into the fire.

'I mean we could start a shop and when the war's over we could sell it and come back here.'

'Come back here! But, son, the house will not . . .'

'I've heard tell of them opening roads in other places, making plans, and then calling a halt to them.'

'I pray God they'll give this up. Maybe, Jim, they'll blot it all out. Maybe after all it was foolish to sell the sheep in haste.'

It wasn't the answer the son anticipated and he added quickly : 'McKeever, I hear, is ready to leave by tomorrow. We'll be the last.'

'McKeever!' and the old man took the pipe from his

lips. 'If McKeever goes we may go. I never knew that man to make a mistake.'

'He's going to live in the city from what I hear.'

'That'll be the first mistake he ever made in his life.'

'We'll never go there, father. Downpatrick's bad enough,' he hedged. 'Still it's a friendly wee town and the fields and the hills wash up close to it.'

'I couldn't end my days in it.'

'Nor could me and Mary. But there's nothing else for us in the meantime but to buy a shop. That's the best proposition I can think of,' and he told his father how they'd need his advice in their buying and selling. 'Whatever we do we must stick together and help one another. We must agree about this while there is still time to do something—no matter how poor it is.'

The old man nodded his head : 'Whatever you do may the good God guide you in it. You have your life to live, and what you think will be good for Mary and the children will be good enough for me.' It was no use at his age, he thought, struggling against his son when there was a coarser authority struggling against all of them.

Within two weeks the son had bought a place in Downpatrick and after removing most of the furniture from the farmhouse he brought in his wife and children. The old man spoke little to anyone.

One day remained to him and he tramped the fields for the last time. The silence of the grave lay over them. Scaffoldings of new huts were being erected on the sea-road, heaps of shavings like the shearings of sheep were blown against the hedges, and the strokes of the men's hammers sounded to the old man like the pulse of his own blood. He reached Dan Mullan's deserted house and as he crossed the threshold, that had no door, a swallow flew out past him. Strange he never noticed them arriving this year, and he now gazed at them skimming swift and sure over the sunny fields. Inside in the house ashes lay on the hearth, and stones and glass littered the floor where schoolboys had broken the windows when taking a short cut across the fields. Up in a corner clung a grey nest of the swallows. They, too, would be cleared out, nothing was safe, nothing left undisturbed. Foolish birds, he said to himself, why didn't you go to the hills, anywhere but here. They'll not let you rest.

On his way back two lorries were pulled up on the sea-road and men were unloading warm-smelling timber. He greeted nobody and nobody greeted him. He looked out to the sea, to black jagged rocks where he often fished years ago. There was no change in them. The rising sea could do nothing to them except wear them smooth. Someday, please God, he'd be here again, indeed he would. The accursed war would be over, the strange huts and the strangers in them would be gone, and tractors would move quickly over the barren fields and crops rise again.

III

When they were settled in Downpatrick the shop closed in the evenings and the father gone to bed, the son used to talk to his wife of the last journey they had made from the house, how his father had padlocked the gate, had his last look at the dark windows of the house, the trees in leaf in the garden and how he had spotted the clothes-line and nothing would do him but open up the gate again and go back for that old bit of rope. They worried about him for he didn't go out much except to leave the two boys at the school in the morning and call into the church beside it. The sheep-dog, too, was listless, its coat lost its shine, and its nose was dry and cracked like a piece of black rubber.

At night the streets were dark and few lamps lighted, and before going to bed the old man listened to the news on the radio, news that might tell him of the war's end. And the mornings were cold and silent. Few lorries or cars were on the roads because of the scarcity of petrol, and it was only on fair days that the old man would rise early on hearing the knocking of farm carts descending to the town and see from his window the sheep on the road with their breaths hanging above them like a sudden fall of sea-mist. And he would hurry on with his breakfast to get out among the lots of sheep that were being sold, the dog barking madly and the old man searching for a familiar face among the groups of farmers. And the seldom time he did spot a friend it was to inquire about the changes that had taken place beyond. Dan Mullan's old house was levelled, he was told, for they were making a road that way. And there were as many new huts about the place as would house an army.

The old man would tell his son about these changes, and tell him that the house must still be standing for nobody had said a word about it. And God would keep her standing he would say to reinforce his faith.

And it was at one of these sheep-fairs that he unexpectedly met Dan Mullan. All day he had been moving around the fair and was returning despondently to the shop when he saw Dan leaning against the counter talking to Jim.

'It's Dan!' the old man shouted, putting an arm on his shoulder and gripping his hand. 'And how are you at all at all?'

'Never better in my life, thank God. And Jim's after selling me as much tobacco as'd do me for a year of wet Sundays.'

'When there's tobacco in the shop there's nobody we'd gladder give it to than yourself.'

'There's not a grain of tobacco to be had in the old place. It was well worth the journey to get it.'

'And how did you get here, Dan?'

'I walked a bit and then got a lift in a cart, and the same man's giving me a lift back.'

'And your old house is tumbled, I hear?'

'She is. Right through her is a tarred road as shiny as the back of a herring. A runaway they call it.'

'I suppose there's great changes everywhere?'

Jim knew what was coming but he had Dan well-primed.

'Aye,' Dan said, staring across the counter at bottles of sweets. 'Big changes everywhere.'

'New huts and sheds?'

'Aye, huts and sheds.'

'I'd hardly know the place?'

Dan took the pipe from his lips, prodding the bowl with his forefinger and struck a match.

'And our house, Dan? Is she—is she in bad shape?'

'No,' Dan said, staring at the lighted match above the bowl of his pipe. 'She's in fine health.'

'Maybe the villains won't touch her. You'll see us back in her some day.'

'It could all be,' Dan said, not looking at him, while Jim stooped below the counter pretending to rummage for something.

'I must be on my way,' Dan said. 'But I'll be back soon again.'

'You're not going till you get something to eat.'

'Eat! Mary gave me a feed that'd do a regiment.'

The old man saw the guilty look in his son's face and scarcely listened to him as he said : 'When Dan called, father, we searched everywhere for you but couldn't find you.

'That's all right,' he said, with a limp wave of his hand.

The old man went out with Dan. They had a quick drink together in a pub, then saw Dan climb into a farmer's cart and set off out of the town.

There was another month to the next fair for he had

marked the date on a calendar that hung in the shop. But he didn't intend to wait that length of time till he'd see again, or maybe not see, someone from his part of the country. Maybe if he walked a mile or so out of the town he'd get a lift in a cart and see the changes that Dan talked about. It didn't matter how he'd get back—he'd get back somehow, he felt.

He said nothing to Jim or Mary, and about two weeks later when the children were in school and the sun shining frostily on the roofs of the houses he set off, the dog with him. He climbed the hilly road above the town and in front of him saw the uneven fields that merged into the hazy distance. He felt in fine form. A fresh breeze was blowing and the falling leaves hopped and flittered like mice, and his dog rubbed the itch off itself against the grassy banks that edged the road, ran back and sniffed his trousers and scampered ahead again.

He had gone nearly two miles when a cart overtook him and left him down a mile from the sea. The sun was setting and the long shadows of trees stretched across the road and bent up on the grassy banks at the other side. The air became colder. He could smell the salt in it and he could hear the dull roar of the sea.

In front of him over familiar fields were outlines of many buildings he had never seen before. But he kept to the road and it brought him among low timbered-huts, huts that swarmed around him on all sides. Concrete paths branched off the road, and at each was an arrow-shaped signpost with printed letters that made no sense. He was in a strange place, but the road led somewhere, and close to a bend in it that he should know so well there was a single-storey building with many windows and doors. Two of the doors were open and the rest were closed, and a man with an aluminium kettle passed by, and another man with shaving-cream on his chin shouted something and closed his door. And now all the doors were closed. But somewhere to the back of that building was his own house and the road to it, but the road that led to that road he could not find. He trudged on, past piles of drainpipes and heaps of sand, and past machines that were like tractors, silent machines tattered with clay and splashed with cement.

And then suddenly he found himself in the cold open air amidst the rushing noise from the sea. He halted and to his left saw the long tarred road Dan had mentioned, and there was a flock of gulls on it and far beyond them were the church and the graveyard, places he had never seen from this part of the sea-road. And then he saw that the sheep-mound was levelled and everything made as flat as the sea. The dog ran away from him and he saw it lapping up water from the steam, the stream that used to flow at the side of his potato field. The dog barked, and with wet paws raced along the smooth tarred road. He followed it till he left the buildings behind him, and then he stopped and gazed towards the place where his house should stand. But it was no longer there, not a stone of it to be seen. There was nothing but a windy plain with neither tree, nor bush, nor cow, nor sheep upon it. Nothing but vacancy, and the sky where the sun had set was a red patch like the glow of a fire on a hearthstone. The dog barked at the gulls and they arose from the black road and passed overhead out to sea. The dog ran back, licked the old man's hands and bounded to the steam again. The old man didn't seem to see it. He trembled and gripped the stick in his hand, his eyes resting on the church and the white headstones in the graveyard.

Six Weeks On and Two Ashore

In the early hours of the night it had rained and the iron gate that led to the lightkeepers' houses had rattled loose in the wind, and as it cringed and banged it disturbed Mrs. O'Brien's spaniel where he lay on a mat in the dark draughty hallway. Time and again he gave a muffled growl, padded about the hall, and scratched at the door. His uneasiness and the noise of the wind had wakened Mrs. O'Brien in the room above him, and she lay in bed wondering if she should go down and let him into the warm comfort of the kitchen. Beside her her husband was asleep, snoring loudly, unaware of her wakefulness or of the windows shaking in their heavy frames. The rain rattled like hailstones against the panes and raced in a flood into the zinc tank at the side of the house. God in Heaven, how anybody could sleep through that, she said—it was enough to waken the dead and there he was deep asleep as if it were a calm summer night. What kind of a man was he at all! You'd think he'd be worrying about his journey to the Rock in the morning and his long six weeks away from her. He was getting old—there was no mistake about that. She touched his feet—they were cold, as cold as a stone you'd find on a wintry beach.

The dog growled again, and throwing back the bed-clothes she got up and groped on the table for the match-box. She struck one match but it was a dead one, and she clicked her tongue in disapproval. She was never done telling Tom not to be putting his spent matches back into the box but he never heeded her. It was tidy he told her; it was exasperating if she knew anything. She struck three before coming upon a good one, and in the spurt of flame she glanced at the alarm-clock and saw that it was two hours after midnight. She slipped downstairs, lit the lamp, and let the dog into the kitchen. She patted his head and he jumped on the sofa, thumped it loudly with his tail and curled up on a cushion. On the floor Tom's hampers lay ready for the morning when the boatmen would come to row him out to the lighthouse to relieve young Frank Coady. She looked at the hampers with sharp calculation, wondering if she had packed everything he needed. She was always sure to forget something—boot polish or a pullover or a corkscrew or soap—and he was always sure to cast it up to her as soon as he stepped ashore for his two weeks leave. She could never remember a time when he arrived back without some complaint or other. But this time she was sure she had forgotten nothing for she had made a list and ticked each item off as she packed them into the cases. Yes, he wouldn't be able to launch any of his ill-humour on her this time!

She quenched the lamp, and returning to her room she stood at the window for a moment and saw the lighthouse beam shine on the clouds and sweep through the fine wire of falling rain. Tom was still asleep, heedless of his coming sojourn on that windy stub of rock. But maybe if the wind would hold during the night the boatmen would be unable to row him out in the morning. But even that would be no comfort—waiting, and waiting, and watching the boatmen sheltering all day in the lee of the boathouse expecting the sea to settle. It'd be better, after all, that they'd be able to take him. She got into bed and turned her back to him, and as she listened to the rain she thought of how it would wash the muddy paw-marks from the cement paths and save her the trouble of getting down on her hands and knees in the morning.

She awoke without aid of the alarm-clock, and from her bed she saw the washed blue of the sky, and in the stillness heard the hollow tumult of the distracted sea. He'd have to go out this morning—there was no doubt about that! But God grant he'd return to her in better form! She got up quietly, and buttoning her frock at the window she gazed down at the Coadys' house. The door was open to the cold sun and Delia Coady was on her knees freshly whitening the doorstep that had been streaked in the night's rain. All her windows were open, the curtains bulging in the uneasy draught. Delia raised her head and looked round but Mrs. O'Brien withdrew to the edge of the window and continued to watch her. Delia was singing now and going to the zinc tank at the side of the house for a bucket of water.

Tom stirred in his bed and threw one arm across the pillow.

'Do you hear her?' his wife said.

'Hear who?' he mumbled crossly and pulled the clothes up round his chest.

'Delia Coady is singing like a lark.'

'Well, let her sing. Isn't it a free country?'

The alarm-clock buzzed on the table and she let it whirl out to the end of its spring.

Tom raised his head from the pillow and stared at her. 'Isn't it a great wonder you didn't switch that damned thing off and you up before it?'

'You better get up, Tom. Delia will think you're in no hurry to take her Frank off the Rock.'

'I'll go when it suits me—not a second faster. When young Coady's as long on the lights as I am he'll not hurry much. The way to get on in my job is to go slow, slow, slow—dead slow, snail slow, and always slow. Do you remember what one of the Commissioners said to me on the East Light in Rathlin? "Mister O'Brien," he said, "there's not as much dust in the whole place as would fill a matchbox." And the secret is—slow.'

'No Commissioner would use such a word as "matchbox".'

'And do you think, woman, that I'm making up that story? What would you have him say?' and he affected a mincing feminine accent : '"Lightkeeper O'Brien, there is not as much elemental dust in the hallowed precincts of this lighthouse as would fill a silver snuff-box." Is that what you would have him say?' he added crossly.

'I don't think he'd pass any remark about dust or dirt.'

'You don't think! You don't think! It's a wonder you didn't think of switching off the damned alarm-clock and you knowing I hate the sound of it.'

She said nothing. All their quarrels seemed to arise out of the simplest remarks—one remark following another, spreading out and involving them, before they were aware, in a quarrel of cold cruelty. She, herself, was to blame for many of them. She should have let him have his little story of 'the matchbox'. What on earth possessed her to turn a word on him and this the last day she'd be speaking to him for six long weeks? She checked a long sigh, tidied the things in the room quietly, and all the time tried to find something to say that would soften her last words to him. She crossed to the window and put her hand to the snib to lower it. Delia was still singing and standing out from the door the better to see the freshly whitened window-sills and doorstep.

'She has a lovely frock on,' she said over her shoulder. 'I never saw her in that before; it fairly becomes her.'

'Didn't I tell you she was married in blue! It'll be the same frock.'

'She has a nice voice.'

'I think you're jealous of her.'

'Hm, I used to be able to sing very well myself.'

'I must say I heard precious little of it.'

'Maybe you didn't! Maybe you'd be interested to know I gave that up shortly after we were married—some twelve years ago.'

'And whose fault was that?'

'Oh, I don't know,' she said, controlling herself.

He pulled the clothes over his shoulder and she pleaded with him to get up and not be the sort that'd deprive another man of even one hour of his leave on shore.

'Is it Frank Coady I'd hurry for! Not me! I'll take my time. I'm over thirty years on the lights and he's a bare half-dozen. He doesn't rush much if he's coming out to relieve me.'

'You can't blame him and he not long married,' she said, scarcely knowing what she was saying as she spoke into the mirror and brushed her hair.

'Last time he came out to relieve me I was waiting for the boat all morning and it didn't come till the afternoon. And what did he say as he stepped ashore? "God, Tom, I'm sorry the boat's late. I took a hellish pain in my stomach and had to lie down for a couple of hours." That's what the scamp said to me instead of offering to give me an extra day on account of his hellish pains. Well, I feel tired this morning and I'm not stirring hand or foot for another hour at least!'

She turned round in her chair from the mirror : 'I'm beginning to get tired of that word "tired" of yours. You were tired last night, tired the night before—always tired. You've said nothing else since you stepped ashore two weeks ago. Tired!—it's not out of any consideration you show me. Going off to the pub of an evening and waiting there till somebody gives you a lift home.'

'And what do you want me to do? What do you want of me?'

'Oh, nothing,' she almost cried, 'nothing! I'm used to loneliness now! I'm used to my married widowhood! In my marriage! You won't come for a game of Bridge of an evening. You're tired—you always say. And if I go you won't wait up till I come back. You lower the lamp and go to your bed. Oh, it's no wonder my hair is beginning to turn grey at the temples.'

'My own is white!'

'What do you expect and you nearing sixty?'

'You're lovely company!'

'Company! Only for the companionship of the old dog I'd go out of my mind.'

'If you'd go out of this room I might think of getting up.'

'Oh, if I'd thought I was keeping you back I'd have gone long ago,' and she lifted the alarm-clock, the box of matches, and hastened from the room.

He stretched his arms and looked at the glass of water on the table. He'd not drink that! The stale taste of it would upset him—and what with his stomach upset and his mind upset he'd be in a nice fix for a journey on the sea. He'd smoke a cigarette—and stretching out to the chair for his coat, he lit one, and lay back on the pillows, frowning now and then at the cold air that blew through the open window. He could hear Delia singing and he wondered if Mag sang when she was expecting him home. He doubted it! She was more attached to that damned old dog, and she thought nothing of walking five miles of an evening for a game of cards and bringing the old dog with her. If she were on the Rock for awhile it'd soon tether her, soon take the skip out of her step. Ah, he should have married somebody less flighty, somebody a bit older and settled, somebody that'd enjoy a glass of stout with you of an evening and not be wanting to drag you over the whole blasted country in search of a game of Bridge.

Downstairs he heard Mag opening the front door and letting out the dog for a run, and he heard her speak across to Delia and say how glad she was that it had cleared up in time for Frank's homecoming. Hm, he thought, she's greatly concerned about the neighbours. He looked at the cigarette in his hand, and from the bed he tried to throw it through the open window but it struck the pane and fell on the floor, and he had to get up and stamp on the lighted end.

His clothes were folded neatly for him on the edge of the table : a clean white shirt, his trousers creased and the brass buttons on his jacket brightly polished. He pulled on the cold, starched shirt and gave a snort of contempt. He wished she'd be less particular—ye'd think he was expecting a visit from the Commissioners on the Rock. Damn the thing you ever saw out there except an exhausted pigeon or a dead cormorant that you'd have to kick into the sea to keep the blowfly from stalking around it. It's remarkable the nose a blowfly has for decaying flesh—flying two or three miles out to sea to lay its eggs on a dead-sea bird. Nature's remarkable when you come to think about it—very remarkable!

Mag tapped the stairs with her knuckles and called out that his breakfast was ready, and when he came down, she glanced at him furtively, trying to read from his face the effect of her remark to him about his white hair. If only she could tell him that she was sorry. But it was better not to—it was better to let it pass and speak to him as if nothing had happened.

'Oh, Tom,' she said brightly, 'Delia was over to see what time you expected to go.'

'And how the hell do I know at what time I'm expected to go? I'll wait till the boatmen call—and to my own slow and unhurried time.'

'She has plenty of paint on, this morning,' she added to restore ease.

'Who has?'

'The old boat, I mean,' she flashed back.

There it was again : they were back to where they started from—chilling one another with silent hostility or with words that would spurt in bitter fury. Oh, she thought, if only he had shown some of his old love for her during the past two weeks they would not now be snapping at one another, and there would be ease and satisfaction and longing in this leave-taking.

She brought a hot plate of rashers and eggs from the range and poured out tea for him.

'Maybe, Tom, I should run over and tell Delia you'll be ready as soon as the boatmen arrive. I'd like to take the full of my eyes of her place as she does of ours. I always think there's a heavy smell of paraffin in her kitchen. Do you ever find it, Tom?'

'That smell's been in my nose ever since I joined the Lights. Do you know what I'm going to tell you?' and he raised the fork in his hand as she sat down opposite him. 'There's nothing as penetrating and as permanent as the smell of paraffin. It's remarkable. It seeps into the walls and it would ooze out again through two coats of new paint. It's in my nose and I wouldn't know the differs between it and the smell of a flower.'

She smiled, for she at that moment caught sight of two cases of Guinness's stout on the floor and she yearned to tell him jokingly that he had a fine perfume for something else. But she repressed that desire and turned to the dog as he laid his nose on her lap. She threw him a few scraps from the table and he snapped at them greedily. She fondled his head and toyed with one of his ears, turning it inside out.

'It's a great wonder you wouldn't put out that dog and let me get my breakfast in some sort of Christian decency. There's a bad smell from him.'

'And you said a moment ago that you could smell nothing only paraffin.'

'Well, I get the smell of him—and that's saying something.'

At that moment the dog walked under the table to his side and he made a kick at it and it yelped and ran under the sofa.

'Come here, Brian,' she called coaxingly, and the dog came out and walked timorously towards her.

'Either he goes out of this or I don't finish my breakfast!'

Without a word she got up and let the dog out.

'Maybe that'll please you,' she said, coming back to the table. 'Anything I love, you despise.'

'That's a damned lie!'

'It's true—and because you thought I was jealous of Delia you praised her.'

'That's another infernal lie!'

'It's too true, Tom. Nothing pleases you—and you used to be so different. You used to be so jolly—one could joke and laugh with you. But of late you've changed.'

'It's you that's changed!'

She took her handkerchief and blew her nose. She felt the tears rising in her eyes and she held her head, trying to regain her self-control.

A shadow passed the window. There was a knock at the door and she opened it to admit three of the boatmen.

'We'd like to catch the tide, Mister O'Brien,' they said, and lifting the hampers they shuffled out of the house.

Tom finished his breakfast slowly and went upstairs. He came down after a short time, dressed, and ready for the road. In a glance she saw that he hadn't a breast-pocket handkerchief, and telling him to wait for a minute she ran upstairs to get one, and coming down again she found he was gone. She hurried after him and overtook him at the iron gate.

'Don't keep me back,' he said, 'didn't you hear as well as I did that we've to catch the tide!' But she held him, and as he tried to wrench himself free she folded the handkerchief into his pocket.

'Tom, don't go away from me like that!' and she looked up at him with an anxious pleading face.

'You're making a fine laughing-stock of me!' he said, and pushing the handkerchief out of sight into his pocket he walked off.

She stood at the gate waiting for him to turn and wave his hand to her but he went on stolidly, erect, along the loose sandy road to the shore. He smoked his pipe, the road sloping before him, its sand white in places from the feet of the boatmen and dark with rain where it was untrodden.

The men were already in the boat, baling out the night's rainwater, and as Tom picked his steps over the piles of slabby wrack on the shore they kept calling out to him to be careful. They assisted him into the boat and he sat in the stern, his legs apart, and his arms dangling between his knees. The boatmen spat on their hands, gripped the oars, and in a few minutes were out from the shelter of the cove and saw ahead of them the black rock with its stub of a lighthouse like a brooding sea-bird. The men rowed with quick, confident strokes, and the boat rose and fell, cutting white swathes on the green sward of the sea.

'Take your time,' Tom said, 'take your time. You're not paid for sweating yourselves. We'll be there soon enough.'

They said nothing, and as they came nearer to the rock they saw the white path curving from the top to the water's edge and saw the waves jabbing and shouldering one another in mad confusion. They dipped their oars now with short, snappy strokes, their eyes on the three lightkeepers who awaited them.

'Ye'll have to jump for it, Mister O'Brien, when we give the word. We'll get the cases landed first,' and while one held off the boat with a boat hook, two stood at the stern with a case waiting their chance to hoist it on to the outstretched hands of those on shore. When the cases were roped and landed Frank Coady jumped and alighting on the gunwale he balanced himself on one leg as lightly as a ballet dancer. 'The fairy godmother!' he said, and folding his arms he spun round on his toe with emphatic daintiness, and then bowing he kissed his fingers to those on shore.

Tom O'Brien lumbered up to him, putting his pipe in his pocket.

'Now, Tom, my lad, let me give you a hand,' said Coady, stretching out his hand to him.

'Get away from me, you bloody fool!' said O'Brien, steadying one foot on the gunwale.

'Be careful now, Mister O'Brien, be careful!' the boatmen shouted. 'Wait till that big fellow passes. Take him on the rise!'

But O'Brien wasn't listening to them. He took his leap on the descent of the wave, missed the path, and was all but disappearing into the sea when the lightkeepers gripped him and hauled him ashore.

'I'm all right! I'm all right!' he said, as they laughed at his soaked trousers, the knee-cap cut and the blood oozing out of it.

'Are you O.K., Tom?' shouted Coady from the boat.

'Ah, go to hell, you!' said O'Brien.

'He's a cranky oul divil,' Coady said to the boatmen as he took off his coat and lifted an oar. 'Now, my hearties, let us see how you can make her leap!' He pulled on his oar with all his strength : 'Up, my hearty fellows! Up she jumps! That's the way to make her skip! I'll leave a pint for all hands in the pub! A pint from Frank Coady!'

Near the shore he turned his head and saw his wife awaiting him.

'There she is, my hearty men! Knitting and waiting for

her darling Frank!' He threw down his oar and perched himself on the bow ready to jump ashore.

'Take care you don't go like O'Brien,' they laughed.

'O'Brien's as stiff as a man on stilts! Here she goes!' and he jumped lightly on to the rock and spinning round he warded off the boat with his foot.

In a minute he was in his wife's arms, and linked together they went off slowly along the sandy road, and for a long time the boatmen could hear him laughing and they knew he was laughing at O'Brien.

Through the iron gate they went arm in arm. Mag O'Brien was outside her house with the dog and as Frank drew near he told her with much joyous relish how Tom had cut the knee of his toursers.

'He wasn't hurt?' she said.

'Hurt—not a bit! He strode up the path after it like a man in training for the half-mile. The only thing you need to worry about is to get a nice patch.' And taking Delia by the hand they swung across to their own house, stood for a minute admiring the whitened doorstep, and going inside they closed the door.

Mag withdrew and sat for a minute at her own window that overlooked their house. Her head ached, and she thought how careless she was in forgetting to pack a bandage or a taste of iodine that he could daub on his bruised knee. One can't think of everything, she said, and she laid her hands on her lap and gazed across at Coady's house that was now silent and still. With an effort she got to her feet and withdrew from the window, and taking a stick she called her dog and set off through the iron gate and away to the shore that was nearest to the rock.

She scanned the rock and the white path down to the sea. If only he saw her and came out on the parapet as he used to do and signal to her she'd be content—her mind would be eased. She sat down on a green slope and waited. There was no stir about the rock, only a gull or two tilting and gliding above the sea. She got up and waved her hand. The dog scratched at the ground, leapt sideways, impatient to be off. She waved again—still there was no sign that she was being seen. She turned and felt the soft wind—it was light and tired : exhausted after its rampage. She stretched herself and stood facing it but it was too weak even to shake her hair. If only it were strong, blowing against her with force she would delight in it. But there was no strength in it—it was indolent and inert, as tired as an old man. She looked once more at the Rock, and seeing a black whorl of smoke rising from it she knew that it was Tom putting on a good fire. He would take a book now, or a bottle of Guinness and his pipe, and after that he would close his eyes and sleep.

The dog barked and ran up the slope after a rabbit. She followed after him and looking to the right she saw the iron gate and the clump of houses she had just left. There was nothing there but silence and sunlight, and behind her the stir of the cold sea.

The Wild Duck's Nest

The sun was setting, spilling gold light on the low western hills of Rathlin Island. A small boy walked jauntily along a hoof-printed path that wriggled between the folds of these hills and opened out into a crater-like valley on the cliff-top. Presently he stopped as if remembering something, then suddenly he left the path, and began running up one of the hills. When he reached the top he was out of breath and stood watching streaks of light radiating from golden-edged clouds, the scene reminding him of a picture he had seen of the Transfiguration. A short distance below him was the cow standing at the edge of a reedy lake. Colm ran down to meet her waving his stick in the air, and the wind rumbling in his ears made him give an exultant whoop which splashed upon the hills in a shower of echoed sound. A flock of gulls lying on the short grass near the lake rose up languidly, drifting like blown snowflakes over the rim of the cliff.

The lake faced west and was fed by a stream, the drainings of the semi-circling hills. One side was open to the winds from the sea and in winter a little outlet trickled over the cliffs making a black vein in their grey sides. The boy lifted stones and began throwing them into the lake, weaving web after web on its calm surface. Then he skimmed the water with flat stones, some of them jumping the surface and coming to rest on the other side. He was delighted with himself and after listening to his echoing shouts of delight he ran to fetch his cow. Gently he tapped her on the side and reluctantly she went towards the brown-mudded path that led out of the valley. The boy was about to throw a final stone into the lake when a bird flew low over his head, its neck a-strain, and its orange-coloured legs clear in the soft light. It was a wild duck. It circled the lake twice, thrice, coming lower each time and then with a nervous flapping of wings it skidded along the surface, its legs breaking the water into a series of silvery arcs. Its wings closed, it lit silently, gave a slight shiver, and began pecking indifferently at the water.

Colm with dilated eyes eagerly watched it making for the further end of the lake. It meandered between tall bulrushes, its body black and solid as stone against the greying water. Then as if it had sunk it was gone. The boy ran stealthily along the bank looking away from the lake, pretending indifference. When he came opposite to where he had last seen the bird he stopped and peered through the sighing reeds whose shadows streaked the water in a maze of black strokes. In front of him was a soddy islet guarded by the spears of sedge and separated from the bank by a narrow channel of water. The water wasn't too deep—he could wade across with care.

Rolling up his short trousers he began to wade, his arms outstretched, and his legs brown and stunted in the mountain water. As he drew near the islet, his feet sank in the cold mud and bubbles winked up at him. He went more carefully and nervously. Then one trouser fell and dipped into the water; the boy dropped his hands to roll it up, he unbalanced, made a splashing sound, and the bird arose with a squawk and whirred away over the cliffs. For a moment the boy stood frightened. Then he clambered on to the wet-soaked sod of land, which was spattered with sea gulls' feathers and bits of wind-blown rushes.

Into each hummock he looked, pulling back the long

grass. At last he came on the nest, facing seawards. Two flat rocks dimpled the face of the water and between them was a neck of land matted with coarse grass containing the nest. It was untidily built of dried rushes, straw and feathers, and in it lay one solitary egg. Colm was delighted. He looked around and saw no one. The nest was his. He lifted the egg, smooth and green as the sky, with a faint tinge of yellow like the reflected light from a buttercup; and then he felt he had done wrong. He put it back. He knew he shouldn't have touched it and he wondered would the bird forsake the nest. A vague sadness stole over him and he felt in his heart he had sinned. Carefully smoothing out his footprints he hurriedly left the islet and ran after his cow. The sun had now set and the cold shiver of evening enveloped him, chilling his body and saddening his mind.

In the morning he was up and away to school. He took the grass rut that edged the road for it was softer on the bare feet. His house was the last on the western headland and after a mile or so he was joined by Paddy McFall; both boys dressed in similar hand-knitted blue jerseys and grey trousers carried home-made school bags. Colm was full of the nest and as soon as he joined his companion he said eagerly: 'Paddy, I've a nest—a wild duck's with one egg.'

'And how do you know it's a wild duck's?' asked Paddy slightly jealous.

'Sure I saw her with my own two eyes, her brown speckled back with a crow's patch on it, and her yellow legs. . .'

'Where is it?' interrupted Paddy in a challenging tone.

'I'm not going to tell you, for you'd rob it!'

'Aach! I suppose it's a tame duck's you have or maybe an old gull's.'

Colm put out his tongue at him. 'A lot you know!' he said, 'for a gull's egg has spots and this one is greenish-white, for I had it in my hand.'

And then the words he didn't want to hear rushed from Paddy in a mocking chant, 'You had it in your hand! . . . She'll forsake it! She'll forsake it! She'll forsake it!' he said, skipping along the road before him.

Colm felt as if he would choke or cry with vexation.

His mind told him that Paddy was right, but somehow he couldn't give in to it and he replied : 'She'll not forsake it! She'll not! I know she'll not!'

But in school his faith wavered. Through the windows he could see moving sheets of rain—rain that dribbled down the panes filling his mind with thoughts of the lake creased and chilled by wind; the nest sodden and black with wetness; and the egg cold as a cave stone. He shivered from the thoughts and fidgeted with the inkwell cover, sliding it backwards and forwards mechanically. The mischievous look had gone from his eyes and the school day dragged on interminably. But at last they were out in the rain, Colm rushing home as fast as he could.

He was no time at all at his dinner of potatoes and salted fish until he was out in the valley now smoky with drifts of slanting rain. Opposite the islet he entered the water. The wind was blowing into his face, rustling noisily the rushes heavy with the dust of rain. A moss-cheeper, swaying on a reed like a mouse, filled the air with light cries of loneliness.

The boy reached the islet, his heart thumping with excitement, wondering did the bird forsake. He went slowly, quietly, on to the strip of land that led to the nest. He rose on his toes, looking over the ledge to see if he could see her. And then every muscle tautened. She was on, her shoulders hunched up, and her bill lying on her breast as if she were asleep. Colm's heart hammered wildly in his ears. She hadn't forsaken. He was about to turn stealthily away. Something happened. The bird moved, her neck straightened, twitching nervously from side to side. The boy's head swam with lightness. He stood transfixed. The wild duck with a panicky flapping, rose heavily, and flew off towards the sea. . . . A guilty silence chilled the boy . . . He turned to go away, hesitated, and glanced back at the dark nest; it'd be no harm to have a look. Timidly he approached it, standing straight, and gazing over the edge. There in the nest lay two eggs. He drew in his breath with delight, splashed quickly from the island, and ran off whistling in the rain.

The Circus Pony

The four children were in the sitting-room, warmly sheltered from the cold wind that was sweeping up in gusts from the lough. Now and again it flung handfuls of hailstones against the window-panes and bumped like a mattress against the gable of the house. Kevin, a boy of ten, was standing at one of the windows gazing out at the dry hailstones as they bounced on the lawn and combed through the chilled trees in the orchard. And with each shower that passed he saw the hailstones gather in the hoof-marks in the fields and lie white as snow on the road that switch-backed across the hedgy countryside.

For awhile he scanned the road for he wanted to be first in seeing his father's car coming from the town and be the first out of the room as it drove into the stabled yard at the back of the house.

His father was to be home before five, and already five had chimed from the marble clock on the mantelpiece, and soon the blue of the sky would darken down for the coming of night and the lights in the farm-houses would shine out across the cold fields.

Of his three sisters Eileen, the eldest, was practising her pieces at the piano, playing softly, and paying no heed to anything else. Rita, with her black fringe broken in places like a comb, was stretched out on the hearthrug with a book propped between her elbows, and Kevin sensed that she was slyly watching him, determined that he wouldn't be first out of the room to greet the car. Joan, the youngest, was kneeling at the sofa with her dolls and scolding her teddybear for having fallen forward with outstretched arms and head touching its legs. 'If you don't sit up straight and have manners like the rest of the children you'll have to go to bed,' she said. 'Do you hear? Now be a good teddy'—and straightening the brass bell on his ribboned neck she stood him soldierly against the sofa and propped dolls at each side to comfort him.

Rita, with one side of her face red and swollen by the fire, glanced at Joan, with unspoken cynicism, and closed her eyes.

'You played with dolls yourself, Rita,' Kevin said, 'so you needn't sneer.'

'I'm not sneering. I'm reading, so mind your own business, Mister Smarty.'

Kevin shrugged his shoulders and turned to the window again. He tapped with his fingers on the window-ledge, beating time to the tune of the piano. Once more he gazed across the fields to the road but seeing its whiteness still unmarked by carlines he knew his father hadn't passed yet. The blue sky was empty of cloud, the fields white except for black patches under the hedges near the roadside. He breathed mist upon the window-pane and as he drew a little man on it with his finger something moving below on the road caught his eye. He put his hands in his pockets and humming to himself he withdrew from the window with a lazy, casual walk. But his manner didn't deceive Rita and she bounced to her feet and rushed to the door shouting : 'Daddy's here!'

'Come back at once!' Eileen ordered as Rita and Kevin struggled for possession of the door-knob. But Rita ignored her, shouldered Kevin aside and was first out to meet the car as it drove up with its roof white with hailstones.

Usually they all fought to get opening the car door but

this evening they held back, fascinated by what was standing up in the trailer attached to the car. It was a black pony, not much bigger than a goat, and it was twitching its ears from the melting hailstones that tickled it. The two yard-dogs were barking furiously and jumping up at the side of the trailer, the children gathering at each side of it, patting the pony's head and picking off the straw and hailstones that were entangled in its mane.

'She's mine, Daddy! She's for me!' Kevin was exclaiming as Joan scampered off to tell her mother to come quick.

'She's not a lady,' the father said as he clouted the two dogs aside and unhitched the tail-board. And there, cradled in yellow straw, stood the whole pony with spills of steam hanging from each nostril. 'He's so small he could hide in a potato bag', the father said, piloting the pony on to the wet yard. The pony stood with patient unconcern, the children hugging his damp cold neck, and the dogs sniffing at the long tail blown sideways by the wind.

'He's for me, isn't he, Daddy?'

'He's for all of you if you behave yourselves.'

'He's one of the ponies we saw in Cinderella', Joan said.

'He's not one of Cinderella's ponies, stupid,' Rita corrected. 'They were all white and he's all black'.

The mother hadn't come out yet to see the new arrival so the pony was led through the back door and down to the warm kitchen, the children skipping with delight on hearing his tiny hooves tinkle on the tiles.

'Glory be to God what have you here!' the mother said, her hands white with flour. 'Where on earth did you pick up that toy?'

'No toy at all,' the father answered, and lifting the pony's long tail he used it to dust the window-sill. 'He can be used for many things, and I believe he can do tricks to no end. He's so clever he can almost tell what you're thinking!'

'I know what I'll be thinking if you don't take him out of my kitchen and let me get the tea ready in some sort of Christian decency,' and she patted the pony leaving a floury mark on his forelock.

'He can sleep in my room in the corner, can't he Mammy?' Kevin was asking but before she had time to reply the father was leading the pony out to the yard again. And leaning into the back of the car he produced another surprise for them : a leather saddle complete with stirrups; and as he strapped it on the pony Kevin and Rita pushed one another and shouted : 'Me first, Daddy. Oh, please, please!' Without a word the father lifted Joan on to its back, and as he led it by the bridle her mother waved out to her from the kitchen window.

Soon they all had rides on it except Eileen and when it came to her turn she refused to take it.

'I'm too heavy,' she protested as Kevin and Rita tugged at her arms.

'She's afraid! Eileen's afraid,' they chanted.

'I'm not afraid.'

'Then why don't you go for a ride?'

'I don't want to.'

'Come on, Eileen,' enticed the father, patting the saddle. 'He's as quiet as a rabbit. He'll not throw you.'

'I'd only hurt him,' she said, disengaging Kevin's hand as he dragged her forward.

To encourage her her father threw his leg over the pony's back and lifted his feet to keep them from trailing the ground. 'Come on, Eileen. Look how he can carry me.' But Eileen could not bear to look at him and she turned and fled into the house, and her father realizing he had distressed her slid off its back and led the pony to the stable door.

'Daddy,' Kevin pleaded, 'get him to do some tricks before he goes to bed.'

'Oh, do, do!' Rita said.

'Some other day but now now. He's tired after his journey and we can't stay out here in the cold all evening.'

'Just get him to do one.'

He didn't listen to them. He lit the hurricane lamp and led the pony out of the draughty yard and into the warm stable. Dolly, the mare, turned her head slowly and glanced sideways at the pony. Beside her great bulk he looked like a strange, undeveloped foal, a foal that could pass under her belly without touching her. He pressed against her front leg and pulled hay from the manger, their shadows staggering on the wall in the light from the lamp. The children eyed him in joyous stillness.

'There's a cheek for you!' the father laughed. 'He's only a visitor—only here on a holiday and he's ready to eat us out of house and home. You'd think he owned the place.'

'Oh, is he not ours for ever, Daddy! Can we not keep him? Can we not buy him?'

'Nothing could buy him. His circus would collapse without him. He has to go back before Easter.'

'Buy why can't we buy him. Why, Daddy, why?' Kevin said, plucking his father's sleeve to attract his attention.

'Hurry in out of the cold,' the father said and bolted the stable door.

It seemed suddenly darker outside, the lamplight flashing on the wet concrete, more stars in the sky and one trembling in the water-trough under the pump in the middle of the yard. An aeroplane zoomed overhead but none of the children looked up to pick out its red and green lights that winked from the wing-tips.

At the tea-table the father related how he had managed to get the pony on loan and how, without fail, he would have to be sent back at Easter to join his travelling circus.

Shaking a finger at Kevin he warned him never to take the pony out on to the road. They could ride him of course up and down to the gate and around the sloping field as soon as the fresh grass began to rise.

He explained how he was to be combed and brushed, how foddered and bedded, and what polish to use on his saddle. He mentioned everything except what mattered most : how you got the pony to do his tricks.

'To-morrow you'll show us—won't you, Daddy?'

'I'll see', the father smiled. 'He mightn't like to do tricks except for payment. If he broke his leg doing a trick, what'd we do?'

'Tell them the truth and don't torment them any longer,' the mother said. She waited but he didn't answer her. 'It's my firm belief you don't know at all,' she added.

'The owner told me he's the cleverest pony in Ireland. He can do everything but talk.'

The mother shook her head and turned to Kevin : 'Go to bed, son. If the pony can do tricks you'll be the one to make him. No one else could do it but you.'

'That settles it,' the father said. 'We'll leave all his capers and performances in Kevin's hands. Here and now we appoint him chief ringmaster.'

When Kevin was in bed Rita came into his room and got in beside him for a few minutes; and they lay and talked about the pony and arranged to call him Dandy. No other name would suit, and if Eileen wanted to change it they wouldn't allow her. He would be called Dandy —and that was that!

Next morning Kevin awoke early. A light covering of snow had fallen during the night and his room dazzled in the reflected whiteness. As he dressed he looked down at the yard to where drips from the eaves drew a dark line on the snow beneath. The pump with its neck maned with snow looked like a stiff little pony drinking at the water-trough; and there were even drips from its mouth tracing little circles on the water, little circles that looped together for a moment and then disappeared. That's how Dandy would drink, Kevin thought; and he wished at that instant to be taking him out just to see how his hooves would print a black letter 'n' all over the surface of the snow.

The latch of the back-door clicked and his father crossed the yard with a bucket, and the two dogs came bounding from the hay-shed and over to the stable-door where they sniffed at the yellow straw that stuck out between the jambs. And in a few minutes the thin snow was patterned crazily with their paw-marks and Kevin knew that before he had his breakfast taken the whole snow would be completely melted from the yard.

He hurried out to school, running ahead of Rita and Joan. He was bursting to tell about the pony, and the boys gathered round him in the playground to hear about it. It was a prize circus pony, he told them, and it could do tricks to no end. What kind of tricks could it do? Oh, all kinds : it could catch the handle of the pump in its mouth and pump up the water. What else could it do? Kevin hesitated, drawing up from his memory tricks he had seen ponies do in Christmas circuses in Belfast. It could beg for bread, he told them, and it could give you its right hoof like a dog giving you its paw. It could walk round on its hind-legs and it could lie down and pretend to be dead. It could add up sums like 2 and 3, and 6 and 4, and tap out the answer with its foot. And if you put coloured handkerchiefs in a box and asked it to pick out a red one it would lift it out with its teeth and drop it at your feet.

He allowed three boys to come home with him after school, but when they reached the end of the drive below the house they heard his dogs barking and refused to go any further till he had locked them in.

He ran up the drive, barred the dogs in a shed, and

whistled to his three friends who stood swinging on the road-side gate. They immediately threw their schoolbags behind the gatepost and raced up to him, and there in the safe silence of the yard they looked over the half-door of the stable at the black pony. It was, indeed, a wee beauty! And then he pointed to the saddle hanging from a peg in the wall. It took their breath away!—the hard shiny stirrups and the leather polished like a new chestnut. They would all get rides on it but not today. He wouldn't be allowed to take it out to the fields till the ground warmed. They would have to wait till then.

He let them into the stable, one at a time, to stroke the pony's head and to feel the steel stirrups and the saddle. In hushed voices they called out : 'Dandy, Dandy!' and to Kevin's surprise the pony cocked its ears and the mare stamped a hind foot on the straw.

'Get him to lie down and die, Kevin.'

'No, no, get him to do a sum.'

'Not now,' Kevin said. 'He doesn't like performing in a stable, and into the bargain he'd only upset the mare.'

At that moment Kevin's mother rapped the window sharply and called him for his dinner.

His three friends scampered off, collected their schoolbags at the gate, and agreed among themselves that it was the dinkiest pony in the whole world.

In the succeeding days the sun lengthened his stride up the sky, the withered grass shrivelled from the rising green in the fields, and the mare and the pony were put out to graze. Kevin and his sisters hurried home from school to ride the pony before the sudden fall of evening and since Kevin hadn't yet discovered how the pony could be enticed to do a trick he allowed the two dogs to accompany him—an unexpressed warning to his school friends not to come into the field. From gaps in the hedge they would safely shout up to him : 'Kevin, make him do a trick . . . Make him do a trick . . . Take in the dogs and give us rides apiece.' And as the pony jogged around, now with Kevin on his back, now with Rita, and now with Joan, bursts of enraged impatience would rush from the outcast spectators : 'Make him gallop ... Ah, he can't run .... You'd get a better jaunt on a donkey.'

'Come on, Kevin, and we'll hiss the dogs on them,' Rita would urge indignantly.

'Pretend you don't hear them,' Eileen would advise.

'They'll change their tune when Daddy shows us how he does his tricks. Won't they Eileen?'

'I'm sure they will.'

But with each day that passed Dandy displayed no mysterious inclination to do anything out of the ordinary. Kevin's friends ceased coming near the field, and in school they often challenged him to race his prize pony against one of their old donkeys. They never wearied in their taunts and mockery.

He grew to hate the school, and one evening as he followed his father round the stables, beseeching him to get the pony to do a trick, his father shouted at him to give over and give his head peace sometime : 'I don't know how he does his tricks and I don't care. You're never satisfied with anything. Away and ride him round the fields and don't bother me any more!'

The next day he didn't go to school. He pretended he was sick. He stayed away for three days. He wanted to forget about the pony's tricks but, when he returned to school, the boys wouldn't allow him to forget. They mimicked him with cruel exaggeration : 'When it begs for bread give it a loaf with jam on it ... It's the cutest pony in Ireland ... It can do sums that'd puzzle the master.'

But the following day, St. Patrick's Day, the miracle happened. Rita and Joan were playing near the orchard, fixing a swing to an ash-bough when they heard in the distance the sound of the Lough Neagh Flute Band, that was marching to the opening of a new sports ground near the chapel. They threw down their ropes, raced to the gate, closed it, and stood up on the bars to await the band.

Kevin was on the topmost bar and by turning his head he saw the band as it came along. The band-leader, out in front in his blue uniform and white gloves, was twirling a pole with a silver knob that caught the sun; and the sound of the flutes and the big drum swamped the noise of the marching feet of the bandsmen and the stumbling feet of the boys who straggled at each side of the road.

The sticks drubbed with furious rapidity on the kettle-drums, and their sounds ribbed out and belaboured the air with a frantic tizzing and frangling that forced Joan to draw back in fear.

The band came abreast of the gate and Kevin looked down at it, seeing the fingers hopping madly on the flutes, and the tiny cards of music with their printed notes like wriggling tadpoles. A boy with spectacles clashed cymbals together, the kettle-drums rolled out once more, and the air pranced with vigorous delight. The band passed the gate, but Joan who was peering fearfully through the hedge screamed out : 'Look! Look what Dandy's doing!'

Near the roadside hedge Dandy was parading round in a circle, nodding his head, lifting his forefeet with exaggerated precision and increasing his pace to the roll of the drums. And then at the sudden cessation of the kettle-drums and at the deep incoming beat from the big drum he rose up on his hind-legs pirouetted and boxed the air.

The roadside hedge was now lined with heads at all levels, laughing and cheering the pony. And the bandsmen marched on, and their leader tossed up his tasselled pole, twirled it dexterously to the cheers behind him and strode ahead with ceremonial pomposity. Dandy followed the band on the inside of the hedge but at the end of the field where a fence blocked his way he halted with one foreleg raised like an equestrian statue, his ears pricked towards the dwindling sound of music.

Tearing across the fields to him came the three children shrieking with delight.

In school the next day everyone was talking about him and of the strange acts he had performed for the Lough Nenagh Flute Band, and after school six or seven boys bolted down their dinner and set off to see for themselves the tricks of this wonderful pony. When they arrived at the field the two dogs were nowhere to be seen and the boys scrambled through holes in the hedge and raced up to Kevin and Rita. Eileen was in the field, too, holding Joan by the hand.

In front of the pony's head Kevin stood with an empty milk can and a stick. He was hammering at the bottom of it, but the pony, with the vacant saddle on its back, was showing no interest in the unrythmical sound. Kevin's friends drew closer to him and pulling pencils from their pockets they held them to their mouths like a flute, ran their fingers along them and began to whistle. Kevin flogged away at the can with his stick. The pony shook itself, turned his back on them and began to graze.

'Dandy!' Kevin shouted, and he jerked the reins till the pony faced them again.

'Ach, he's stupid,' one of the boys said with disgust.

'He's the cutest and cleverest pony in Ireland.'

'Everybody knows it,' Kevin said.

'Make him give you his paw.'

'Make him lie down and die.'

'Make him do some damned thing and not keep us standing here all day.'

'Nobody's asking you to stand here all day!' Rita said pertly.

'Give us a ride on him.'

'We're not allowed to,' Rita said, tossing her head.

The boys laughed and elbowed one another, and one of them lifted a lump of sod and threw it at the pony.

'Just for that we'll not get him to do any tricks!' Kevin said.

'You don't know how! You don't know how!' they chanted.

'Don't I! I could get him to do thousands of tricks!'

'Get him to do them! Get him to do even one!'

'Go on home out of this,' Eileen said, noticing that Kevin was nearly in tears.

'We'll go when we're ready. You think because you're at a convent school you can order us about,' one said, and they giggled and stumbled against her.

'I'll get the dogs and they'll fix you!' she said, and on hearing this they fled down the field and on to the road where they hung about, shouting and jeering through holes in the hedge.

Rita lifted Kevin's stick, marched over the pony and mounted him smartly. She tapped him with the stick and he suddenly took fright and galloped down the sloping field. She was bounced about without grace or rhythm. She tried not to scream, and as she was joggled off she held on to the reins and was dragged along the ground.

She heard a volley of cheers from the road and she scrambled to her feet and lashed out at the pony with her stick. And suddenly the pony rose up stiffly on its hind legs, grimaced horribly, the silver bit in its mouth and grass between its teeth.

'Rita! Rita!' Eileen yelled as she and Kevin ran down to her. Eileen snatched the stick and broke it in two, the pony still pirouetting, and breathing with a fearful choking sound.

'Now you see how you get him to do his tricks! You see it now!' Eileen said in a broken voice. 'It's horrible,

horrible,' she cried, waiting for the pony to cease its painful caperings.

'There, Dandy! That'll do! Down, please, down!' she said soothingly, and at that moment she saw the fear of punishment in its dark eyes, saw the cruelty that produced circus joys.

At last, exhausted, the pony placed its forefeet on the ground. Its sides heaved rapidly and little patches like snow gathered at the corners of its mouth. It stood still, subdued, motionless with expectant fear.

Rita was crying and rubbing her knee, and Joan was helping her to pick the pieces of crushed grass from her frock.

Kevin stared dumbly, now at the pony, and now at the broken stick lying at Eileen's feet. He was thinking of something, something that puzzled him. But what it was he did not know.

Mother and Daughter

The old lady in the private ward had expected her married daughter since two o'clock and since it was now nearing four her scrap of patience had begun to shrink. Propped up in bed with a woollen lavender cap on her head like a tea-cosy she stared aggressively at the closed door and saw in its dull glass panels the blurred figures of nurses passing to and from the public ward. She could hear their bantering voices raised in laughter and she grew more annoyed and tried not to listen to them. They didn't give her much of their time, she reflected; indeed, she could be dead and gone for hours before they'd discover it. No one gave her a moment's notice, a moment's consideration. She supposed private ward meant privacy—it also meant neglect where she was concerned! And wasn't she old, and wasn't she paying through the nose for this private room, a room furnished like a Victorian hotel. And then there was the bell-push looped round the rail of the bed which she was to ring if she wanted anything. Oh, she liked that part of it! How often had she rung and rung and no one had paid any heed to it. And it wasn't that the bell was out of order for the seldom time they did answer if they did so immediately.

But today you'd think they had gone on strike for she was sure she had a calloused finger from ringing the same bell. She was sure too her temperature and blood pressure were rising steadily.

She turned around and eyed the bell, and to appease her annoyance she pressed it again and heard it cheer itself hoarse in some part of the building. But no one answered it. Laughter came again from the public ward, and she wondered what they had to laugh at and maybe some poor patients needing a little rest or, God help them, lying at death's door. Come to think of it she herself would have been much better off in the public ward instead of being cooped up all alone like a Victorian dowager. For one thing she'd have had loads of company and loads of attention, and strange people traipsing in and out, and so many of them on visiting days there wouldn't be enough chairs for them to sit on and they'd have to perch on the edge of the bed or stand leaning over the bedrails. Her daughter wanted her to go there in the first instance and it was a pity she didn't heed her.

But what on earth was keeping her so late today after promising she'd be here at two. Oh, the same girl never hurried except when it suited her! Selfish, selfish—that summed her up.

She sighed resignedly and glanced at the chart hanging over the aluminum rail at the foot of the bed. She saw the black peaks and hollows on it like an outline of the Rockies and wondered what it all meant.

The door was knocked and a nurse slipped in.

'Did you ring, Mrs. Collins?'

'On and off for the past three hours.'

'And what may I bring you or do for you?'

'You're all doing for me if you'd like to know! But I'll lodge a complaint to the doctor in the morning.'

'There are other patients in the hospital, too, Mrs. Collins.'

'I don't want any impertinence, any back answers, either from you or anyone else. I'm in a private ward and I'm not paying dear money to be scolded or abused. All I ask is a little attention, a little consideration—half of what's given to the patients in the public ward would suffice.'

'We're doing our best for all, Mrs. Collins. We're short-handed.'

'You may be short of hearing too, but you're not short-tongued. Would you please hand me my knitting from the top drawer there.'

'Let me prop you up on the pillows properly, and get you ready for your daughter.'

'I'll require that if she comes. What sort of a day is it outside?'

'It's snowing steadily and the roofs are covered white.'

'Snowing! Why wasn't I told so that I needn't expect my daughter. That's another instance of the silent cruelties of this place.'

'It only came on a short while ago.'

'You've an answer for everything, my girl. Perhaps you'd refill my hot water bottle before my poor feet are frozen stiff.'

'With pleasure, Mrs. Collins,' and the nurse fished it out from under the bedclothes and held it in her arms as she would a baby. 'I'll be back in a minute,' and she smiled and hurried from the room.

Mrs. Collins eyed the hand of the clock on the dressing table. She'd time that lassie.

Five minutes passed, and then ten.

She'd give her two minutes more before she'd poke the bell. Who ever heard of a quart of warm water taking ten minutes to boil! I suppose she'll tell me the gas is on low pressure or the electric has failed because of the snow.

She lay back on the pillow and drew her feet up from the cold regions of the bed. She shivered. She'd get that blade to take her temperature when she'd come back! She stared at the clock and then gripped the bell-push and gave the button a prolonged squeeze.

At last someone stood outside the door and she could distinguish the white uniform of the nurse. She was talking to someone. Perhaps one of the young student doctors. The impudence of that one! The bottle would be cold by the time she had finished her tête-a-tête.

The door opened and the nurse came in backwards.

'I thought you'd never come and my poor feet frozen.'

'Was I long, Mrs. Collins?' the nurse said brightly as she stowed the bottle beneath the blankets.

'It's a pity I'm not a young man and not an old woman. I'd get full value out of my private ward, I'm thinking.'

'You needn't expect your daughter today. By the look of it the snow's on for the whole evening.'

'Indeed I'll expect her! My daughter has a sense of duty. From an early age she was taught to have consideration for others.'

'If your daughter's wise she'll stay at home,' and the nurse stood at the window and gazed down at the snow obliterating the car tracks that led from the gate. 'I wouldn't be at all surprised if the buses cease to run.'

'You're very comforting, I must say.'

'If you turn your head, Mrs. Collins, you can see the snow on the roofs. It must be an inch or so deep, for the outline of the slates is blotted out.'

'If you give me the hand mirror I might be able to see the snow without getting a crick in my neck.'

The nurse lifted the mirror from the dressing table, blew her breath on it, and wiped it with the corner of her apron.

'Well now, Mrs. Collins, what do you see?'

'I can see nothing except an old woman who's badly failed since coming to this inhospitable place.'

'Indeed, you're looking well.'

'If you had seen me 20 years ago you would have seen a very beautiful young woman. Anyone would tell you that who knew me.'

'I'm sure.'

'The way you say it you're not so sure.'

'You're still handsome. One hasn't to go back 20 years to find that out.'

'Why don't you sit down, nurse, and relax for a minute or two.'

'You never saw a nurse sitting except at meal times. We're always on the go.'

'If you are it's not to this room you do be going. It's little attention I get from any of you.'

'If you needed attention we'd be in and out 20 times an hour.'

'So I'm not sick at all—is that the next of it!'

'Oh, no, Mrs. Collins,' the nurse smiled. 'You're still far from well. But you're no longer on our danger list.'

'If I were no longer on the paying list I'd be happy.'

The nurse rearranged a few bedraggled chrysanthemums in a vase at the window and on looking out saw Mrs. Collins's daughter and grandchild coming through the gate.

'I must go now,' the nurse said without telling her the good news. 'Just ring if you want anything.'

Left alone the old lady lifted the mirror and watched the snow falling. Yes, the nurse was probably right. Her daughter wouldn't come, and that snow would be a convenient and plausible excuse. She lay back and shut her eyes, the hand mirror face downward on the eiderdown.

The door was knocked and in walked her married daughter with her six-year-old child. She carried a bunch of pink chrysanthemums that were moist with melted snow, and before greeting her mother she placed them upright in the wash basin.

'Are you asleep, Mother?' she whispered, stooping over the bed to kiss her.

'Sure you know I never sleep. And what possessed you to take Mary out with you on a day like this.'

She's in one of her tantrums, the daughter said to herself, and called on God to give her patience during the visit. Slowly she took off the child's cape and hat and draped them over the back of a chair, and sitting beside the bed she told her mother she looked greatly improved since her last visit.

'I may look it, Lizzie, but I don't feel it,' and thereupon she launched into a litany of complaints about the nurses' inattention and the cold meals served up to her. The daughter sighed and patted the eiderdown, but after listening to another volley of complaints she said quietly, 'I wish, Mother, you weren't so querulous. The poor nurses are doing their very best.'

'Oh, if that's the mood you're in, my lady, you shouldn't have come out to see a sick and lonely old woman.'

'I don't like to hear you complain so much, that's all.'

'I'm not complaining, I'm just stating the bare facts.'

The child, not interested in their talk, wandered about the room, pulled out drawers in a bureau and was surprised that they contained nothing, only a blue sheet of paper flattened tightly to the bottom. Some of the drawers stuck as she was closing them, and one rather stubborn one she pushed so vigorously that a statuette of Our Lady rocked precariously on top of the bureau.

'Now see what you have done, Mary. Come here beside mother and keep your hands to yourself.'

'It's high time you corrected her. She's a little curiosity box.'

'Why do your teeth click, grandma, and mine don't?' the child said, staring at her grandmother and the lavender cap on her white head.

'What does the child say?' the old lady asked, leaning forward with a hand to her ear.

'She wants to know if you like her new blue cape.'

'She doesn't suit blue. You should have bought her a red one or a black one.'

The child, dashed, hid herself at the back of her mother's chair, but after a few minutes they had forgotten about her and she once more roamed about the room.

'John has a bit of a cold,' the daughter said, mentioning her husband's name for the first time. 'But he'll be up to see you soon.'

'I suppose he's overworked these days,' the old lady said with false sweetness, aware that sloth was John's predominant passion.

The daughter clasped her hands on her lap and yearned to be out once more in the wide airy spaces of the street. No matter what she said she failed to make contact or break down the tension that divided them. Everything was going wrong : the snow, the long wait for the bus, and then the failure of the visit. She sighed, and as the daylight shrank from the room she switched on the light and drew the curtains.

And then suddenly there was a rumble and stumble on the floor, for the child had opened a press and out spilled bananas, turning black, and oranges and apples.

'Well, well, well, that's a spill! There's no peace with that child. Leave her at home next time you call.'

The mother stooped and pressed the burst bags of fruit into the press, and red in the face from exertion and anxiety she sat down and breathed audibly.

'You should give some of that fruit to the nurses. The bananas, I may tell you, are turning black.'

'They may turn pink for that matter. I wouldn't give the same nurses the skin of an orange if it were to save their lives.'

'The nurses! The nurses! Can you not stop pecking at them sometime. They're an overworked and underpaid body if you'd like to know.'

'That's right, stand up for them against your poor tortured old mother.'

The child by this time had discovered a small box of Turkish Delight that had fallen at the side of the press and she was poking a finger on the sugared jelly and licking it when her grandmother spotted her.

'My God, look what she has now!' she shouted. 'My Turkish Delight, the only sweet that lies at peace on my stomach. Hand them up this instant!'

She took the box and pushed it beneath her pillow, and the child, almost in tears, stood beside her mother and asked if they weren't going home soon.

'In a minute or two, Mary. Be patient, girly.'

'You should have left her at home instead of hauling her out through all that snow.'

'If I had left her at home you'd have asked why I didn't bring her. Oh, you haven't spoken a kind word to her since we came in.'

'I didn't wish to interrupt her plundering expeditions.'

'She didn't get much plunder as far as I can see!' the daughter flashed back, and then in an instant regretted it. The old lady closed her eyes, turned her head away, and raised a hand in a gesture of dismissal.

Quietly the daughter put on her own coat and then buttoned on the child's cape.

'Mother.'

'Let me sleep, please.'

She pulled on her gloves : 'Mother, I forgot to tell you that Sally Morgan is getting married.' She paused, but her mother didn't stir. 'She's getting married to . . . You'll never guess?'

The old lady shrugged her shoulders, but did not speak.

'We're going now,' her daughter went on. 'Is there anything special you want and I'll have it sent up to you?'

'Nothing, thanks. My needs are few. But do try to be in better form on your next visit.'

'I'll try, Mother,' she said, taking the blow. 'The snow and the long wait for the buses have put my nerves on edge, I suppose.' She stooped and kissed her mother.

The old lady looked fixedly at her; she wanted to ask her whom Sally Morgan was going to marry but she held back, stiffening herself against the impulse to please. But when the goodbyes were said and the door closed she felt her pride uncoiling in a long irregular line of angry discontent. She rang the bell. She wanted the nurse to call them back. She rang again and again but no one answered her.

Meanwhile her daughter had reached the outside gate, glad to be out in the free falling snow. She held Mary's hand tightly, but the child disengaged it, and while waiting for the bus watched the flakes turning her cape white.

They boarded the bus and the child knelt up on the seat, wiped the mist from the window with her gloved hand and looked out at the streets that were as white as the bed in the hospital.

'Why was grandma cross?' she asked.

'She wasn't cross, child. Your poor grandma is sick.'

'And what made her sick?'

'She's growing old.'

'And what made her old.'

'Turn round and sit on the seat like a good girl.'

The child turned around from the window and sat on the seat, watching the flakes of snow melt on her blue cape and dribble on the floor.

At the centre of the city they had to change buses and stand in a queue. Beside them was a café and when the door opened the warm burnt smell of coffee rushed out into the cold air.

'Come, Mary,' the mother said, and taking the child's hand she led her into the café and sat at a round table near the window.

'And now, Mary, what would you like to eat?'

'Sweets, Mammy. Turkish Delight like grandma's.'

'We'll see.'

The mother rose from the table, crossed to the counter, and carried back two cups of tea, a few biscuits, and a small box of Turkish Delight.

The child smiled, took the box, and pushed the inside out like a matchbox. Lying closely side by side were cubes of coloured jellies dusted with fine sugar.

'You take one first, Mammy,' the child said.

'The mother smiled, and to hide the warm tears of joy that rose up beyond her control, she lowered her head near the box and rhymed :

Eena, meena, mina, mow,
Catch a sweetie by the toe,
If he squeals let him go,
Out you must go.

She prized out a cube with her fingers and put it in her mouth. The child smiled, but seeing the tears in her mother's eyes she said :

'You're crying, Mammy?'

'The cold is making my eyes watery—that's all.'

'But it doesn't make my eyes watery,' she said, lifting out a sweet and putting it in her mouth. She smiled and looked at the large window that was misted over except for drops of water wriggling down the pane and leaving clear tracks behind them.

Is she thinking of her grandma and the hospital? the mother wondered, staring at her child.

The child swallowed the remains of her sweet and smiled :

'Look, Mammy, the window's crying. Look at all its tears.'

The Schooner

It was August and very warm; Terence Devlin, a boy of eight, was leaving the city with his father for a holiday on the Island of Rathlin. It was early morning when they walked to the station where porters were rim-rolling milk cans along the empty platform. At Ballymoney they had to change and wait for a long time for the narrow-gauge train to take them to Ballycastle. That train was very small and the people seemed too big for it; steam dribbled from all parts of the engine and Terence held on tightly to his father for he feared that it would explode at any moment. The wooden seats in the carriage were rough and hacked with names, and they hurt the backs of his knees. In the floor boards there were wide slits and through them could be seen the sharp stones which lay between the sleepers. The train shook violently and Terence's teeth rattled in his head and the suit-case fell off the rack on to the floor.

'I hope you'll not be sea-sick in the train,' his father smiled to him, and put away the paper he was trying to read. When the train slowed down he would shout out to his son the names of flowers and mosses that grew on the rocky embankments. But to amuse himself Terence dropped cigarette-cards between the floor boards and spelt out words that were pencilled on the ceiling. His father told him to try and sleep and not be straining his eyes reading words that were written by bad boys : 'It's the like of those things that bring a bad name on the country. I hope, Terence, you'll never scribble in a railway carriage.'

After that Terence dozed off and when he awoke he was in Ballycastle. There was the smell of turf and the air was heavy with heat. Down past a siding they walked where the wooden sleepers were sticky with oil and smelt sharply of tar.

They stopped at a shop and Terence bought ice-cream, a wooden spade, and a red bucket with black letters : *A Present from Ballycastle.*

They took the long road to the sea. Men with twisted towels round their necks passed them. Blinds were pulled down in the big houses and on the lawns old ladies sat on deck-chairs under the shade of red umbrellas. Terence shook a pebble from his sandal, and Mr. Devlin walked on, fanning himself with his hat. The big chestnut trees that lined the road were stiff with heat, but under the leaves flakes of shadow quivered. The tarred road crackled as a motor raced by, then a drove of cattle came up, their hooves sticking in the tar, their dung-caked sides as dry as the bark of a tree.

'If we get weather like this, Terence, we'll not know ourselves on the way back.'

While Mr. Devlin went to inquire about the boat Terence leaned over a sun-warmed wall and saw below him boys and girls playing tennis. Boys hung blazers on the net-posts, hitched up their belts, and through the sun-sifted air came the cord-rattle of tennis balls hitting the net and nearby a lazy plunge of waves falling on a curve of sand. Idly he picked moss out of the crevices in the wall, and then a finger flicked his ear and he turned to see his father smiling down at him : 'We'll go over to the quay now, the boat's going to the island shortly.'

Alongside the quay lay a boat, a brown sail wrapped round the mast and old motor tyres hanging over the sides. The out-going tide had left pools of water on the quay, and strands of seaweed had entangled themselves under the mooring rings. At the end of the quay three boys were fishing for fry and behind them sat glass jamjars filled with shining water and green moss. Terence yearned to take off his sandals and dabble his scorched feet in the pools, but already his father was handing the suit-case to a man in the boat and he joined him to see the cargo being taken aboard : two bags of flour, a tea-chest filled with loaves and covered with sacking, a coil of barbed wire and two panes of glass.

There were five islanders, some tall and awkward-looking, standing loosely as if they were ashamed of their height. Terence and his father sat in the stern; the tyres were pulled in, and one of the crew lifted an oar and pushed the boat out from the quay. The gunwale was warm and blobs of resin had oozed out of the wood. The sky was clear, the sea smooth and a fierce sun striking into it.

Ballast stones were dropped overboard and Terence saw the water fizzle white and felt splashes of salt on his lips. Four oars were fixed between the thole-pins and dipped into the water simultaneously; drops dripped from the blades, whorls were left by the thrust of the oars, and looking back Terence watched for a long time the wrinkled patches of water fade into the smooth sea. He could still hear the dull thud of waves on the sand and he wondered in what part of the ocean the waves were hatched. He was going to ask his father, but he was now pointing out Fair Head to him and telling him a story about beautiful children who had been turned into swans and how for many lonely years they had wandered about this sea.

Far out from the Head two steamers were very black [illegible] seemed to float in the sky. Gulls flew close to the [illegible] their reflections clear in the smooth water; puffins stood up and flapped their wings, or to escape the boat they arose in a flock and flittered the top of the water with their feet. But for all the rowing the island seemed to draw no nearer. It lay spread out in front of them, its white cliffs like a row of teeth, and to the right its black cliffs polished by the sun.

'Now, men,' said Mr. Devlin, 'I could give one of you a spell,' and he took an oar, splashed awkwardly, and broke the rhythmic dip-and-lift which had fascinated Terence.

'Don't dip the blade so deep,' said one of the islanders, and with great patience he showed Mr. Devlin how to feather his oar. In no time the sweat was gleaming on Mr. Devlin's forehead, and soon he had to take off his coat and waistcoat.

'It's tough work when yer not used to it,' said a little brown-faced man who was rowing near the bow.

Mr. Devlin grunted and turned around to look at the island : 'I'm damned if we're moving at all. I thought we'd row over in ten minutes.'

'No, nor in ten times ten minutes. 'Tis a long pull —eight miles across.'

Mr. Devlin puffed loudly and his oar left no whirling holes in the water. Presently he gave up : 'Gentlemen, I think I've worked my passage,' and he sat in the stern and his hands fell limply on his lap.

Later Mr. Devlin began to ask questions about the island, and the boatmen answered him, and in his own mind he began to plan what walks he would take during his fortnight's holiday. Terence picked out the white houses that lay in the scoops of the hills and the square-towered church and graveyard that edged the coast. Now the boat was passing between two quays, and a clump of men with their hands in their pockets gazed at the boat as she came in. There was a strong smell of rotting seaweed rising from the bay. White ducks were dozing on the grass above tide-mark; along the strand a man in his shirt-sleeves was carrying two cans of water, and a bare-footed boy was throwing a stick into the water for a black dog to retrieve it.

Terence and his father made their way up the stony quay, past a rusty winch and a broken boat with green-scummed water. The houses were low and slated, and one of them with two sentry-box porches had its name in Gaelic letters printed on a thin board.

'This is our ticket,' said Mr. Devlin, and they walked up a gravel path towards it.

A tall woman in black opened the door : 'Welcome to the island,' she said. 'We didn't see the boat comin' in or faith we'd have sent Paddy down to meet it . . . Come on in. Annie's bakin' and the place is a bit throughother.'

They were in a warm kitchen with a shining range, and Annie was turning farls of bread on a griddle and hurried to greet them : 'Ye must be famished with the hunger. I'll not be long gettin' the things on the table.'

The two women were dressed alike : black blouses with high collars, grey hair topped with big combs, but Annie had on a spotted apron, and two broad rings were grooved so tightly on her finger that the flesh was swollen at each side.

'Lizzie,' she said quietly, 'take their things up to the room,' and she stood beside Terence, holding his cap and stroking his fair hair.

A door opened on the opposite side of the kitchen and Paddy slouched in, his sleeves rolled up, a rough-haired terrier at his heels. The dog began to bark at the strangers and Paddy swiped at him with his hat : 'Chu, you brute! Chu, Bumper, and have some manners!'

He shook hands with Terence and Mr. Devlin, and then sat beside them on the sofa, idly picking clay from [illegible] fingers with his thumb nail. Annie moved from the [illegible] to the griddle : she was very quiet, shadow-like, her elastic-sided boots making no noise, her eyes withdrawn and brooding.

The kitchen was big : a wag-at-the-wall ticked loudly, and in the deep window that faced the sea there was a white spool, a yellow tape, and a calendar with its leaves curled and a red outline of a fish on all the Friday dates.

'Ye got a lovely day for crossin', so ye did,' put in Paddy. 'it was a long pull, but ye had the tide with ye.'

'There wasn't a ripple. I never saw the sea so calm,' answered Mr. Devlin.

Annie scraped the griddle noisily with a knife and swept the scrapings in to her hand with a goose's wing. Paddy crossed and re-crossed his legs.

'The sea was like oil,' continued Mr. Devlin, trying to make conversation. 'And it was covered with birds.'

Annie dropped the knife, and then quietly opened the back door and went out.

Paddy got to his feet, glancing at the door : 'Calm weather is scarce in these parts. There wasn't an air of wind the past two days.' He stuffed a piece of twisted paper between the bars of the grate and lit his pipe. 'Weather like this would do no good; the soil's as dry as snuff.'

Annie came in and Paddy added hurriedly : 'And, Mr. Devlin, while you're here you must get a night or two's fishin'. The sea's thick with fish.' He hitched his belt : 'I'll leave ye now till you get your tay. I've a field of purties I have to weed.'

Bumper slid out from under the table, but when he saw Lizzie enter with an old raincoat he wagged his tail.

Lizzie smiled at Terence and turned to the dog : 'Bumper, are ye goin' to Ballycarry?' The dog jumped into the air three times, ran under the stairs and came out with a basket in his mouth.

Terence laughed and said to his father : 'Could I go to Ballycarry?'

Lizzie folded her arms : 'Ah, child, it's too far. It's away up in the mountains, but if you come here next year you'll be a big boy and I'll take you and Bumper up to Ballycarry.'

Kneeling on the sofa he watched through the window : Bumper walked in front, the basket in his mouth; Lizzie followed, a gleaming can hooked to her elbow. They passed behind a limestone wall, her head bobbing up and down; then the road swept alongside a hill, dipped into a hollow and they were lost from sight.

For the next two days while his father tramped the island gathering specimens of wild flowers Terence played about the house waiting for the time when Bumper and Lizzie were to set out for Ballycarry. On the third day he was strolling about like that when he saw the door of a little lean-to lying open. Cautiously he went in and found Annie sharpening a knife on a hone. She didn't hear him. The sun was shining through a small window and the shadow of a bush flickered against the pane. It was cool and quiet, and broken cobwebs dangled from the bare slates. There was no sound except the rasp of the knife. He was going to go out when he saw on a shelf a model schooner with brown sails, brass hooks and rings, and underneath the tail-shaped stern the painted name : *Windswept*.

'Oh,' he said, 'who owns the lovely boat?'

Annie started at the voice and turning round she saw him tapping the deck and moving the sails backwards and forwards. Silently she stared at him. He stroked the hull with the palm of his hand and toyed with the helm.

'Who owns it?' he asked again, his eyes wide with anticipated joy.

For a moment she was rigid, then she relaxed, and a [illegible] of brooding doubt spread across her face. Again he tapped the deck, and her expression changed to one of patient sadness.

'You can play with it,' she said, almost in a whisper. 'You can play with it, and Paddy will show you how to trim the sails.'

In a minute he was out and off to the shore. Paddy met him : 'Where are you goin' with that? You can't have that!' he said in great surprise.

'Annie lent it to me. She said I could play with it and you could fix the sails for me.'

'Wait now a minute. Don't go away.' And Paddy hurried up to the little lean-to. Annie was standing in the shadow of the doorway and came to meet him. Both raised their hands and waved to Terence to go on. Paddy followed him, thinking how long the little schooner had remained on its stand and how for many years Annie had polished it : 'It's curious the changes that come over people—changes ye'd never dream of.' And he rubbed the back of his neck with his hand.

He sat on the beach stones above the little bay, took the schooner on his lap and showed Terence how to use the helm : 'Turn it to the left when you're sailin' her with her bow pointin' to the house.'

Terence took off his sandals and placed the schooner in the water. All her sails tightened in the breeze and her brass rings glinted in the sun. Annie saw it from the door : the rust-brown sails, the wet-gleaming hull, and the silver flakes of water skimming from the bow. Paddy walked along the strand, then a disturbing thought whorled in his mind, for he wondered was the ship water-tight after her years on the stand. He called to Terence to bring it up to him, and with his ear to the hull he turned the boat up and down; he could hear nothing except a slight seed-rattle of a chip of wood inside her.

'She's as tight as a pig-skin—a lovely boat! She's the

girl can whip along in a thin breeze .. Take good care of her.'

All that day Terence played with the boat, and in the evening after his supper Annie, with a thin shawl on her shoulders, came down to the shore to bring him home. The sun had gone down and the water was darkened by a chilly breeze .

He shouted : 'Look now!' as the boat tore across the bay and a knife-curve of water rolled white at her bow.

'Come, Terence, it's gettin' late. What'll you father say if you're not in bed when he comes back from fishin'?'

She waited on the shore road for him, and presently he came floundering up the loose stones of the beach with the schooner hugged to his breast. He was out of breath and full of joy. Then he saw that her eyes were wet.

'What's wrong?' he asked.

'I was just thinkin',' she answered clumsily and tried to draw his attention to a shower of moths that flickered over a field of beans.

'But why were you crying?' he persisted.

'I was thinking of the boat. It was my husband made it.'

'And will he make one for me?' Terence asked eagerly.

'Indeed, he'd make you one.'

'And when will he make it? Where is he?' he kept repeating. 'Where is he?'

She stood still on the road : 'When he comes back, please God, he'll make you one.'

'And when will he be back?'

'It's getting cold. We must hurry now,' she evaded.

There was great heat in the kitchen from the humming range. The curtains were drawn and the oil lamp lighted. Terence was allowed to look at the book of flowers that his father had already gathered and sometimes Annie would bend over him, take from her apron pocket a sugar lump and put it in his mouth. He loved this time of the evening with no one in the kitchen but the two of them, and even Annie, herself, looked forward to this hour before his bedtime. He was great company. Sometimes he would thread her needle and she would sit and watch him, her hands loosely on her lap. She would given him milk to drink and he would sit near the range feeling the heat on his knees and hearing outside the unhurried breath of the waves. Then when he would nod his head in sleep she would light a candle and bring him to his room. She used to allow him to keep the schooner under the dressing-table, but one evening when she heard him coughing she stole upstairs and found him asleep on the floor beside the schooner.

The next day she feared he would have a cold, but he set off with his father to swim and later she coaxed him to sit with her in the sunny field at the back of the house. The foot of the field had a crop of blossomed potatoes and Paddy was spraying them with blue stone and from where they sat they could hear the spray rattling like hail on the leaves and see the blue sheen of it as it dried in the sun. Butterflies pirouetted over the field and Terence caught one and placed it on the palm of his hand. The powder from its wings clung to his fingers and he put the butterfly on the ground and it began to struggle up a blade of grass.

'It'll never fly again,' Annie said to him as she looked over the calm sea. 'The powder on its wings means as much to it as wind for the sails of a boat.'

The remark hurt him and he watched with growing sorrow the blade of grass bending under the weight of the ungainly butterfly and how brilliantly white its helpless wings shone in the sun.

Paddy came up to them for a drink from the can of milk, his eyebrows and clothes covered with a fine blue dust. One foot crushed the butterfly, and Terence was going to cry out when he noticed that Annie was engrossed in her knitting and didn't see what had happened. Presently she got up and went inside to get ready the tea, leaving her rug and knitting in the field.

'Do you know what you've done?' said Terence to Paddy. 'You've tramped on a butterfly and killed it.'

'And sure what sin is there in that?' replied Paddy, noticing how his lips quivered. 'Sure they only live for a day and some of them don't live as long as that—the swallows and thrushes snap them in two while you'd wink.'

Paddy lay back and pulled his hat over his face. Terence took off his sandals and felt the soft grass on his bare feet. He closed his eyes from the glare of the sun and thoughts of cool things stirred within his mind—moss floating in a jamjar, drops on the blade of an oar, and rain washing the powder from a butterfly's wings. He sat up and on gazing at the sea he saw that a schooner with all her canvas out was passing up the sound.

'Oh, Paddy, look at the lovely schooner like Annie's!'

Paddy took the hat from his eyes and stared at the ship : 'It's not often you see them about now. They're a grand sight. That one is only drifting up there on the first of flood—there's no wind for her.'

'I'll run and tell Annie.'

'Come back here and let her make the tay,' and he rose to his feet. 'Come on with me and spray the spuds.'

Terence hesitated : 'Let me tell her!'

'You'll not!' Paddy said sharply. 'Do what I say!'

Reluctantly Terence came over to him, and slowly they walked down to the barrel of spray, Paddy looking now and again at the schooner and calculating how long it would take her to drift out of the sound, knowing also that she would surely drift back again if the wind did not rise during the night.

He got Terence to pick up the flinty pieces of limestone that lay between the drills and to search under all the leaves for the Queen of the butterflies. 'And you'll know her,' says Paddy, 'by her wings, for she has one wing of pure gold and one of shining silver, and if you find her you'll be able to sell her for hundreds of pounds.' And while Terence searched, Paddy sprayed until the schooner had nearly passed up the sound. Then clapping the dust from his hands he went to the top of the field and gathered up the rug and the knitting.

When they came in Lizzie and Bumper had arrived from Ballycarry, and Bumper lay at the open door in the sun snapping at the flies. The cement floor was cold under Terence's feet and Annie made him sit down at once and put on his sandals.

As the evening grew old the warmth left the earth and the potato-blossoms closed up and drooped their heads. In the kitchen a warm silence crept into all the corners and a trapped fly buzzed madly in a web.

During the night a rainy storm blew against the house, and in the morning when Terence wakened he saw his father standing at the window : 'Terence, boy, it's like a winter's morning. The summer's finished and tomorrow, if the boat can leave, you'll be on you way back again.'

Two conflicting thoughts encumbered the boy's mind : a desire that the storm would last a long time so that no boat could leave; a desire that the storm would die at once so that he could get sailing the schooner before he left. At breakfast he heard Paddy assure his father that the storm would last no time and that it would blow itself out before night.

When Annie was making the beds Terence went with her and from the window they looked out upon the bay. Ducks and hens sheltered under the boats that were hauled up on the grass. The wind flayed the water into jagged peaks; waves tore between the two quays, crashed on the strand, and sent jabbling fingers amongst the stones on the beach. Gulls rose from the stones and tipped the waves before they broke. Tangles of brown sea-wrack curved the bay and clumps of it floated in a solid mass.

'Oh, look!' Terence would call out as a big wave struck the quay and burst in snowy spray. Annie would cross to the window and share for a moment the vigorous joy of wind-torn water.

When she had the beds made Terence shyly plucked her apron : 'Could I have the boat?'

'Terry, you have no sense—one wave would smash the riggin' and leave it like a butterfly that had lost its wings,' and she stroked his head and smiled at him meekly.

'Well, could I have it after awhile if the wind goes away?'

'We'll see.'

In the afternoon the wind had fallen, and late that evening when the wind was exhausted and only a glimmer of it flicked across the bay Terence pleaded again for the boat.

Annie laughed at him : 'At this time! Ye'd be frozen down on the shore.'

'Ah. please, I'll be going away in the morning.'

'But sure you'll be back next year and you can sail it till your heart's content.'

'Just one more for the last,' he kept pleading.

Paddy was dozing on the sofa, and Lizzie was trying to read a paper in the light from the fire, but did not raise her head.

Terence asked again.

'All right,' said Annie, and getting the key she went out for the schooner. 'Just sail her once. Darkness will soon be here.'

The chilly water took his breath away as he set the rudder and let the boat slide from his hand. As he ran along the cold strand he could see the sails black against the light from the water. He sailed her back across the bay again and then heard Annie call to him from the lighted doorway.

'I'm going now,' he shouted, waiting for the boat to come to shore. But then something happened. The schooner stopped, tangled in a clump of floating wrack. He waited for her to free herself. Then he noticed she was slewing round. He clenched his hands and involuntarily pressed his feet into the sand. The sails flapped, caught the wind, and she headed out between the two quays towards the open sea. He began to cry. He ran to the first quay. He skinned his legs as he climbed on to it from the strand Annie called to him again, but he didn't hear her. He lifted a boat-hook that lay on the quay and peered at the waves that slopped in amongst the stone steps. Once he thought he saw something pass at great speed, but he wasn't sure. Backwards and forwards he ran from one quay to the other like a dog that had lost his master. Desperately he searched, lifting up sand-soaked tins and flinging them into the water. His throat was scorched. He heard Annie call to him from the shore : 'Terence, Terence, are you there?'

He went back to look for his sandals. The incoming tide had almost covered them. Annie came down to him over the beach stones : 'Where did you get to?'

He couldn't answer. When she came close to him she saw him without the boat and heard him sobbing.

'Where's the boat?' she asked.

Through his tears he told her how he had fixed the rudder and how the boat had caught in wrack and had turned round. She stood beside him and squeezed his head against her breast : 'Don't cry, Terence. Don't take it so ill.' A deep shivering convulsed her and she squeezed him with great possessiveness and stroked his hair.

Paddy and Lizzie were seated at the fire and looked questioningly at Annie when they saw Terence's scratched legs and the tears in his eyes.

'He lost the boat,' said Annie, 'and he's broken-hearted.' An awkward silence fell. Lizzie poked the fire and Paddy fumbled in his pockets.

'Wash your face and legs and don't let your father see you in that state,' and she made much noise under the stairs getting a basin and a towel. Lizzie and Paddy said nothing.

'Don't cry; sure that could happen to anyone?' she said, drying his face and legs.

'It was the rudder . . . I fixed it right and it caught in seaweed on the way over and turned round.'

'They're a misfortunate thing to put on any model boat,' put in Paddy.

Annie stared at him, and he went out and walked about until the lamp had been lowered in the kitchen and all had gone to bed.

In the morning it was raining heavily and some sheep that were to be taken to the mainland stood on the quay bleating and calling to others that were being driven along the strand. Dogs were barking, and drenched men with no overcoats shouted to one another. Mr. Devlin heard them as he washed, and he hurried Terence out of bed and carried down the suit-case to the kitchen.

'There'll be a bit of a jabble on the sea,' said Paddy as they sat down for their breakfast. 'It's raining badly and I have an ould bit of a sail you can spread on your knees.'

He looked out of the door : 'Yiv plenty of time—eat yer fill. They're carrying the sheep to the boat but I'll not bring my three down till yer nearly ready.'

Through the open door they could hear the melancholy bleat of sheep and see a loose web of rain wind-trailed across the bay.

Annie was quiet : 'You'll send Terence back next year for all his holidays. Paddy, there, could meet the train at Ballycastle.'

'Would you like that?' said Mr. Devlin.

Terence nodded his head. He wanted to talk about the schooner, but he knew if he opened his mouth no words would come.

Paddy carried the suit-case to the boat, Lizzie and Bumper followed. In the porch Annie held Terence's hand : 'It won't be long till next summer and if God spares us all you'll be back again.'

He couldn't look up at her and he noticed that stains of salt water had whitened the toes of his sandals.

'Goodbye', she said and watched them go down the gravel path.

They clambered into the wet-soaked boat and a man rubbed a seat for them with a wisp of straw. When Paddy had tied the legs of his sheep he carried them abroad and sat beside Terence and Mr. Devlin. The sail was unrolled from the mast and blobs of rain-water fell from its folds; it filled in the breeze and the driving rain rattled on it like countless bird-pecks. Lizzie stood on the quay with her arms folded and Bumper ran around shaking the rain from himself. From the porch Annie waved to Terence; the tears came to his eyes and he pretended to look for something under the seat. The water slid past the boat, her bows crunched into the waves, and Terence raised his head and scanned the shore for the schooner. But he could see nothing, only black rocks with waves jumping over them. Slanting clouds heaved up against the hills and stitched the valleys with rain. The houses were falling behind and soon there would be nothing to mark them except the big telegraph pole above the post-office.

The wet sheep lay on yellow straw, steam was rising from them, and now and again with the pitch of the boat they tried to scramble to their feet. The rain wormed down a bit of sail that was spread across Terence's knees, and Paddy tried to light his pipe by pulling the edge of the sail over his head.

Terence now searched the sea, and his gaze was so

prolonged and intense that Mr. Devlin nudged Paddy : 'He's looking for the boat.'

'Ach, God knows where she is by this time,' replied Paddy.

'Would it cost much to replace it?'

'Ach, Mr. Devlin, it's not the cost that matters—it's what it meant to Annie,' and he bent confidentially to Mr. Devlin. 'It was her husband that made it thirty years ago. It was a model of his own ship and since he went away she cleaned and polished it. It held raw memories for her!'

'Where is he now?' Mr. Devlin asked.

'He never came back. They were married in June and early in September of the same year he went away and she never saw him again.'

'Were they . . . happy?'

'Happy! . . . He was a ship's carpenter—a fine lump of a fella—and made every stick of furniture that went into their house. They lived at Ballycarry on the east side of the island. We still have the house, but she never goes there now . . . She still thinks he'll come back.'

'And will he, do you think?'

Paddy shook his head : 'He'll not, poor fella. I think he's drowned.'

Terence's eyes were on the sea, but sometimes when a sheep would move he would stretch out his hand and pat its wet head. Paddy spoke in a low voice, but Terence wasn't listening to him.

'They spent three happy months together on the island,' continued Paddy. 'His ship was bound for Canada for a load of grain. It left the Clyde and it was to pick him up passing the island. He was on the look-out for it and when it came into the sound they sent a small boat ashore for him. But at night the wind had fallen and the schooner was becalmed.'

Mr. Devlin noticed that his suit-case was lying flat and

the rain was creeping into it, but he did not move and inclined his head nearer to Paddy's.

'Annie kept her light in the window and at dawn she was down on the shore looking out at the great schooner. She waved, knowing he'd see her. The next day the ship was still there. It was a day like the one you met coming to the island—terribly warm. But during the night a wind sprung up and she saw her lights moving out of the sound . . . That was the last she saw.'

'And what happened?'

'The boat nor crew were never heard tell of . . . She always felt that he was alive and that he'd come back . . . She's got very old waiting . . . For awhile she used to walk about the house at night, opening and shutting doors. But she got over that.'

'It's a great pity Terence lost the little schooner on her. She shouldn't have lent it to him.'

'Ah, Mr. Devlin, she has great liking for your son —great liking. And you'll have to send him back next summer. The loss of the wee schooner may do good, for it's gone now and she won't be cleaning it and thinking . . . There was times I wish somebody had stolen it.'

They were both silent. Three big waves hit the boat and sent the spray flying over them.

'Man, Terence,' said Paddy, 'if the wee schooner met fellas like that they'd make short work of her. But, maybe, she's ashore somewhere below the white rocks.'

'And will you look for her?'

'I will, I will,' said Paddy, trying to relight his damp pipe. But the abstracted way he answered made Terence feel that the schooner meant nothing to Paddy; he knew he would never see it again and that he'd have no schooner to play with when he'd come back next year.

After Forty Years

In spite of the hard rain that struck against the windows the air in the compartment was warm and comfortable, and as the almost empty train rattled and shrugged through the night-dark countryside the woman in the corner seat persisted with her knitting, and her husband, whose eyes were at their fading stage, tried to read, the book shuffling on his knee despite his efforts to steady it. They were alone, and in the rack above them were two suitcases, a man's tweed hat and a fishing rod in a brown canvas cover. They spoke little to one another, but when the train would draw up at a station the woman would raise her head from her knitting and say : 'Where are we now, John?'

Her husband would glance at his watch and tell her, and a few minutes later the porter, passing outside on the platform, would confirm in a loud voice the name of the station John had already announced. Then the guard's whistle would flare into the night and with a jolt the train would move off again, the lights from the platform shining for a moment into the passing compartments.

The woman would again take up her knitting, the man his reading, their reflections in the dark windows keeping abreast of them.

The train gathered speed, and the book balanced on the man's knee shook so unsteadily that he turned down a page at the corner, closed it, and folding his arms leaned back against the headrest. His wife looked across at him, at his white hair, and at his pale face that would after a couple of weeks' fishing, turn to the brown colour she loved to see on him. It would be their first holiday together since he retired from teaching, a holiday she allowed him to arrange without even one suggestion from herself. And to her delight he chose the last week in August and the first week in September. The hotels would be quieter then, and their sleep undisturbed by the restless holidaymakers who crammed the hotels from July to the middle of August. Yes, the hotels, like the train, would be comfortably empty.

The train slowed down, and when it stopped the man awoke and heard the rain slapping from the roof of the carriages and strolling down the pane. He yawned and rubbed his eyes.

'Where are we now, John?'

He didn't answer, but with a folded newspaper wiped away some mist on the window and peered out at a dreary platform where rain-soaked advertisements glistened in the lights from the train. He waited for the porter to call out the name of the station, but evidently, the train being almost empty, the porter didn't consider it worthwhile.

He stood up to open the window and his wife ordered him to put on his hat or he'd catch cold. He obeyed her, crammed it on his head, and on opening the window a few drops of rain flew into the compartment. The air was cold against his face, the wet platform deserted except for the guard and porter, and beyond the white arrowpointed palings that marked the end of the platform a red light of a signal glowed in the darkness.

The train hissed, the guard raised his flag and blew his whistle, and as the train slowly passed the end of the platform John saw the name TOOME in large white letters against a black rectangle. For a moment he caught sight of the lights in the village and he continued to lean out, his wife calling to him to close the window at once. But he didn't seem to hear her, and in a minute the train was thundering over the bridge across the river and a solitary light on its bank scribbled its reflection on the cold water.

'John!'

His wife rose, pushed him to the side, and heaved up the window on its leather strap.

'Do you want to get your neuralgia back again?'

'That was Toome!'

'I don't care if it was Buckingham Palace. You'd no call to stand there so long. Such a miserable place to be gazing out at!'

'I once lived there myself, Margaret,' he said quietly.

'No,' she said, incredulous, looking across at him.

'Yes, but only for a short spell. It was my first teaching post.'

'You never mentioned that before. And how long have we been married—40 years. Well, well, why did you never tell me you taught there?'

'No reason whatsoever, Margaret. It just didn't occur to me—that's all.'

'Come now, John. You must have had some reason. What was it?'

She had suddenly become animated, and she rolled up her knitting and put in inside a magazine beside her.

'There's some reason why you have kept it from me all these years. Come now—out with it like a good man!'

The train whistled sharply and sped on into the night, and the man, no longer interested in his book, closed his eyes, a sad expression aging his face.

His wife leaned forward and touched his knee.

'What made you leave? Was it too lonely for you?'

'It wasn't lonely. I liked it. I loved the fishing and the boating. I used to spend hours on that river we're after crossing.'

'And you left because you liked it. That doesn't make sense to me. Come now : why are you so secretive about it? I must know.'

'There's nothing to tell, Margaret,' he said, giving a sad smile. 'It's over 40 years ago since I was there and there's really nothing to tell.'

He shrugged his shoulders and leaned back against the seat.

'Where you in love—is that it?'

'I don't think it was that.'

Over the long flat stretch of land the train stretched out eagerly, their shoulders jogged and swayed, and the back of the man's head rubbed against the leather head-rest. Toome was a long way behind now, the Toome that he had known : its river that unrolled like a web of ice over the falls and then broadened itself into little lakes which he had explored in the long days of a summer gone by.

'John, there's something on your mind about that place and I must know.'

'Wouldn't it be better to let the past lie? Please, Margaret, don't go on.'

'So you have a past! And all our married years I have never known.'

He smiled and remained remote from her, wrapped up in his own secret memory.

She opened her handbag, touched up her face, and for a moment the compartment smelt like a bathroom. They had no children and in spite of her years she wore young clothes to set off a figure that was still attractive. The train would be late arriving in Derry where they would spend the night before setting out for Donegal in the morning.

'And she was handsome—this early sweetheart of yours?'

'I didn't say she was a sweetheart. It's you that has said it.'

'I suppose she was handsome if you fell in love with her. Was she a teacher in the same school?'

'She was. She was a few years older than I was and she was the principal. It was a two-roomed school.'

'And you proposed to her and she refused and you left in affront.'

'No, Margaret, she was already married.'

'That makes it more interesting.'

'It makes it more sad.'

'Why are you so aggravating? You want me to tell what I know nothing of.'

'You're making a brave hand at it, I may tell you . . . Sure it doesn't matter now. It's all over and done with, some 40 years ago.'

'I love you so much I could still be a bit jealous,' she said with unconscious irony. 'You gave me to understand I was the first girl you ever fell in love with.'

'And so you were. And that's the truth.'

'How annoying you are this evening! Perhaps you'd like us to return and spend a few days fishing in Toome?'

'No, I wouldn't want that. I have never been back there since I left.'

'Is she still alive, this person?'

'No, she died shortly after I left. She died in a boating accident. I read an account of it in the papers. May God have mercy on her.'

He glanced away from the interrogating eyes of his wife and looked at the window, at the blurred reflection of his hands, his white hair, and his face.

'She was married to a man years older than herself. When he had drink taken he was rough with her. For some reason she used to confide in me. She felt, I suppose, that I would understand and wouldn't gossip.'

He raised a hand and it fell limply on his knee.

'Ah, Margaret, we'll let the long past lie in peace,' and he shook his head with a sad gesture.

'So she confided in you because she trusted you. And here we are at this distance on in our lives and you've no wish to confide in me.'

'After 40 years I'm not absolved from the promises she made me give her. Time should not erode one's faith and trust. She asked me never to repeat what she had confided in me, and I have never done that.'

'I'm not asking you to. But surely you could tell me what she looked like and how she dressed.'

He paused and gave a resigned smile.

'She had black hair. It was very black and her eyes were a kind of grey or green. She usually wore a blouse and skirt. Sometimes a yellow blouse or a white or green one and a rose pinned to it.'

'For a young lad just fresh from the training college you took good stock of her.'

'I see her in memory only. It's your questions that bring it all back.'

'But what reason had she to confide in you?'

'I don't know. There were only the two of us all day long in the school. I suppose the poor girl was lonely and had no one else to talk to. It was her confidence in me that made me leave and look out for another school. At lunch-hour when the children were out in the playground and the two of us were drinking tea she used to roll up her sleeve and show me the dark bruises on her arm and the marks of a man's fingers. I had pity for her. I often yearned to put my arm round her to console her.'

He shook his head : 'There are times, Margaret, when sympathy and pity can be dangerous.'

'You'd think, John, you had never heard of the ninth commandment.'

'Yes, it was that that made me leave so suddenly. I knew it couldn't go on . . . When I saw the tears in her eyes it took my whole strength to hold back from lifting her hand and kissing it . . . And the way she could sing.

I used to pause in my work to listen as she led the children through *The Last Rose of Summer.* That song, God knows, is sad enough. But the way she sang it made it the saddest of all songs.'

The train whistled and the wheels rocking unevenly over a roadcrossing drowned his voice, and he clasped his hands and dropped them between his knees and fell silent.

'Go on, John, let me know more about his woman. Did you ever kiss her?'

'Never!'

'On your oath?'

'Why do you pester me, Margaret, over an incident that happened 40 years ago? I didn't kiss her, I tell you!'

'But you would have liked to!'

'She was another man's wife. But I was horrified one day on our way home from school to see chalked up on a stone by the roadside our initials : J.T. loves M.D. Mary Doyle, you see, was her name. I rubbed the initials off with a sod I pulled out from the ditch. She laughed and said : "Aren't they the little divils!" I was more distressed than she was. But she really loved the children—you could sense that by the way she spoke to them. Even when she was angry they sensed her love for them. "How would you like to see your own mothers' names chalked up on gateposts?" she said to them. And do you know, Margaret, they loved and respected her so much it never recurred again. I was glad of that. If her husband had heard of it or seen it God knows what he would have thought.'

A sudden squall struck the windows, and the rain rattled against them as hard as pebbles. He sighed, stared at the swaying leather strap of the window, and went on.

'And yet there was nothing wrong in this friendship of ours. She it was who opened the school early in the morning, and in the afternoon, because my road led past her house, she used to ask me to wait for her while she tidied up the rooms. And the silence then, with the children gone, was like no other silence I can remember ever since. The clock, which we couldn't hear all day, tocked on the wall like the blows of a mallet. And around us were the empty desks, a boy's torn cap on a peg, and on one wall the large map of Ireland patched with sticking-plaster. I can see it all as if it were yesterday. She seemed reluctant to leave it. It was like home for her, I suppose. And after she had powdered her face at a little mirror no bigger than a postcard I held her coat for her as she struggled into it. She used to smile at that and say in her musical voice : "Oh, how kind you are." And then on our way home we talked about books. She liked reading but her husband didn't. I used to lend her books, but her husband burnt one in one of his rages and she refused after that to accept another. That was kind of her—always thoughtful of others. I remember one day on going home like this she saw a child's ribbon in the dust of the road, and, instead of kicking it with her toe, she lifted it and put it in her handbag, and in the morning she had it washed and ironed and sought out its owner. Isn't it sad, Margaret, a young wife like that to be drowned in a boating accident?'

'From what you say I gather you were in love with this Doyle woman. Were you?'

'No, I don't think I was. Ah, how could I be and she with a wedding ring on her finger.'

'And was she in love with you, do you think?'

'I don't know that either. She never did anything or said anything to express it as far as I know.'

'Would you have been shocked if she had done something?'

'I intended for my own soul's sake to leave. She was already married. I used to find myself thinking of her—thinking of her coarse husband and how cruel he was to her, and she so gentle. In the mornings her eyes were often red from crying. But I never let on I noticed it. And then as the day progressed she became happier, younger looking. The presence of the children she loved had that effect on her. She was happiest when she was teaching or when she was drying the children's wet coats by the fire in the school. And how brisk and graceful she was in all her movements.'

'Did you ever meet that husband of hers?'

'I did, but I never exchanged many words with him. He had plenty of money but he squandered it foolishly. And to see her coming from Mass on a Sunday, so light on her feet, and he with his coarse laugh, his heaviness, and his bulging waistcoat, I always wondered why she had married him.'

'And not you—is that what you thought?

'Even if she had been single I couldn't have married her. I had nothing to marry on. It took all I earned to pay for my lodgings. But, anyway, the thought of marrying never entered my head. It wasn't that, Margaret : it was just that she was miserable and I wished, in what way I don't know, that she could be happy.'

'What did she say when you told her you were leaving?'

'She was sorry I was going. She pleaded with me to change my mind. And on my last day she gave me a fountain pen and asked me to write to her.'

'And you wrote, of course?'

'No, Margaret. She asked me to address the letter to the school.'

'A woman can speak for a woman, John. This Doyle one was in love with you! God only knows what would have been the end of the story if you had remained on.'

'I may not have met you.'

'And would you have regretted that after what you have told me?'

'Margaret, what are you saying? After 40 years you

don't doubt my love for you. I never used the pen she gave me. It's the one that's lying in its case in a drawer at home.'

'You never used it! I always wondered why you never gave that pen away—you that's so generous, generous to a fault. It was a keepsake, I suppose. That's why you never parted with it. It reminds you of her.'

'I once offered it to you. But you wouldn't use it. Its nib was too broad, you said.'

'But you could have given it away.'

'That never occurred to me. But I'll give it away when we get home. I could give it to some jumble sale or other.'

'You're saying that now, because I have caught you out. You may hold on to it for another 40 years for all I care.'

He shook his head, leaned forward, and patted the back of her hand. She shrugged away from him and took up her knitting.

'The poor girl hadn't much of a life.' he went on. 'She died, you might say, before she had begun to live. And her death . . .'

'I don't want to hear another word about her!' and plucking at her needles she upset the ball of wool and it rolled off the seat on to the floor. He retrieved it and left it on her lap.

'Their boat was found capsized. A sudden squall must have struck it. The mainsail, you see, had been tied—it said so in the papers . . . Her husband's body was washed ashore on one of the islands, but hers was never found . . . never found . . . It was probably carried down the river in flood and into the sea . . . To think she died like that, and she so young, so light on her feet, and so thoughtful of others . . . God have mercy on her.'

He leant back against the headrest and closed his eyes. His wife continued her knitting with grim speed, the train rattling loosely on its journey through the night.

Stone

A small flame trembled above the turf on the hearth, shrivelled and disappeared, leaving a cord of smoke ravelling itself in the wide chimney. Old Jamesy Heaney sitting with his hands on his knees, his shoulders drooped forward, waited for the fire to light. At his feet lay his black and white collie, her forepaws in the ashes, a wet nose on the flags. The closed door was slitted with light, and through the nests of cobwebs on the deep window came a blue wintry brightness. It was cold.

The old man prodded the fire with a twig and presently it fluttered into life. He'd made a sup of tea before going to the village and while the tin boiled he'd get ready his eggs. He stood up and hobbled to the dresser. The dog got up too, leaving a damp mark on the stone where her nose had lain. She yawned and sat back on her haunches watching the slow fumbling movements of her master.

He was a small grasshopper of a man, withered and worn, and cold to look at. His clothes were patched and tattered, and round the loose soles of his knobbly boots he had lapped coils of wire which now and again rasped on the stone floor. As he lifted a can from a nail in the wall the dog jumped around him and ran towards the door. Old Jamesy paid no heed to her, and went on wrapping hen-eggs carefully in paper and placing them in the can. He had only seven eggs this evening; the frost must have put the hens off their laying. He'd have another look outside; maybe there'd be one or two more.

An icy wind blew into the cottage as the collie crushed out in front of him, sending panic into the fluttering hens. Jamesy yelled at her in a voice that broke sharp on the lean hollows. He crossed to the hen-shed; it was a rickety place patched with the coloured lids of tin-boxes. Near it was an ash tree trodden bare round the trunk where the hens and goat lay of a hot summer day under the quivering shade from its little leaves. Now it was deserted, a red flannel rag caught on the black twigs, making a leafy sound as the wind strummed the branches. Jamesy shrugged his shoulders as he looked at the frost on the rag and at the misty vapour that smothered the nearby sea; the devil take it for frost, good hot male given to the hens—and no eggs. When he came out from the shed they began clustering at his feet and he whished them away from him.

'It's the last yellow male ye'll get for awhile, me ladies. Content yerselves on the nest or go and scrape and fend for yerselves. Be off now!'

The black tin was spluttering and hissing on the fire when he came inside. He gripped the handle with his coat and snuggled the tin on top of a hot, crushed turf.

Jamesy lived alone and made his own meals. He was the last of the Heaneys left on the island. Sitting now with the mug between bony hands, his grey beard on his chest and his long hair fringing his coat collar, he looked like an ancient prophet. The dog nuzzled under his arm and awakened him from a dream, whereupon he threw the dregs of tea at the back of the fire and lifted his can and stick.

He turned the key in the door, tried the latch a few times, and clattered across to the road. From the first crest on the road he would stop and look back at his cottage. From there he would see the smoke tearing itself from the stump of a chimney; the loose black thatch with the eaves as ragged as an old brush; and the tree near the gable where he himself sat in the cool of a summer's evening enjoying the hush around him and the sleepy stir of the sea. And from these his gaze would slowly turn to the potato patch, black and bare now with withered stalks strewn about.

It filled him with pride to look down at the closed cottage impersonally, as if the house belonged to someone else and he envying the owner as he passed on the road. It was a wild, draughty place surely, but it was far from the villagers with their taunts and jibes; and he loved it, loved every stone of it. And then it was his own; there was sweet comfort in that thought.

Gripping his stick he turned his back reluctantly. His old goat, shrunken with cold, me-eh-eh-ed as she saw him disappear over the hill. Jamesy walked firmly on his heels, knees slightly bent, his stick jabbing the road. The air was keen and blue, long streamers of cloud frozen to the sky, the scattered bushes naked and empty of birds. A frost-fringed stream trickled darkly at the side of the road, and now and then the ice that patched the hoof-marks splintered under Jamesy's stick. He wore no overcoat and as he walked along his shoulder blades knuckled under his jacket. He kept an even pace. Once the dog thudded after a rabbit, and returning licked Jamesy's hand, and trotted proudly in front.

At the top of the graveyard hill he stopped for the second time, his breath gusty and misty in the air. Satisfied that there was no one about he shuffled over to the rusty iron gate of the graveyard and lifted the loop of wire that held it. The dog waited on the road beside the can.

Jamesy didn't go in to pray. He stood a short distance from the gate looking thoughtfully at the wind-streaked grasses, and at the lumpy graves with their small wooden crosses and slabs of rock. There was only one headstone;

a large Celtic cross of blue granite, its panelled arms and shaft decorated with an interlacing design. On its thick base in large block letters was the name of one man, McBride; a bachelor like Jamesy himself. With head to the side Jamesy looked at the gravelled grave with its neat plinth and iron-railings, and then up at the huge stone dusted with frost. Everyone in the island referred to it as the McBride monument, and they talked about it from time to time. A sadness chilled Jamesy. It was a lovely grave; a sweet grave, near the road and looking down on the fistful of houses that was the village. But as he walked over to his own naked patch of ground warmer feelings began to stir within him.

Last week he had bought the site from the priest, a piece of ground eight feet by twelve, and he smiled to himself as he recalled the priest's words : 'It'd take less than that to hold your bones, Jamesy. You'd think you had a big family;' and his own reply : 'There's nothin' like havin' a roomy place when a body's dead.' Poor Father Brady, little did he know what he wanted it for; little did he know!

As he measured the plot with his stick grunts of satisfaction came from him, and occasionally he would glance furtively over the low graveyard wall. He stood back, screwing up his watery eyes to the sky where his imagination etched the stone that would mark his own grave. It'd be two feet higher than the McBride stone; he'd see to that.

Out on the road again his mind began to play with the familiar thoughts, and an exultant feeling flamed within him. It would be his stone that the people'd talk about when he'd be gone; and visitors to the island would look at it and read the name, JAMES HEANEY; a great man they'd whisper amongst themselves! He rolled the thought over in his mind, holding on to it. His body quivered as the solid reality of the stone possessed him.

And then he stopped dead in the middle of the road, and the dog, ears cocked looked up at him sideways. Crashing into his mind there came something more than the talk of the people about his headstone; his name was going to live; it would live forever in solid stone.

'Stone is the only lasting thing in life,' he breathed aloud; it bates all, he never thought of that before. He held his breath, as if to calm his mind, to allow it to gather the sweet breeze of thought and unfold its joys to him. Stone is lasting : all life ends in death, but stone lives on. It was more lasting than all their children. They needn't chaff him any more about his name dying with neither chick nor child to leave behind him! They needn't mock him any longer! There they were as usual, the three of them—Joseph McDonnell, John Joe McQuilkin, and Johnny John Beg. He'd have it out with them this evening.

The three old men were smoking in the lee of a gable, watching the sea break on the shore, and the children playing. They were silent, their jigging feet knocking chips of limewash from the wall. But when Jamesy approached, the children raced off into their houses, and the old men began to talk excitedly amongst themselves. In his pride Jamesy walked past them into the shop.

Quietly he placed his can on the counter and sat down on an empty onion-box. There was a great sense of ease and comfort in the box-cluttered shop, with its fat meal bags, the clock ticking, and a warm smell of baking bread coming from the kitchen. He sat still, drawing a sweet warmth from it, afraid to budge lest the shopkeeper would come at once to serve him; it was like being under a clucking hen, he thought. Presently a chair moved and the clip-clop of feet approached; Jamesy tapped the counter with feigned impatience.

The shrivelled shopkeeper entered, her hands white with flour.

'That's a sharp evenin', Jamesy,' she greeted.

'Tis that; we're goin' to have a hard winter, I'm thinkin'.'

She looked over the counter at his face; his eyes were blurred, and the left one had a red, drooped lid, with water dribbling from it making a streak in his white beard.

'You're eye's brave and angry lookin' the day,' she sympathised. 'Why don't you try the boracic; a tuppenny packet would make it as clean as a whistle.'

'Ach, I'll not bother now, sure it's no trouble to me at all; and in the good weather me eye's as dry as withered seaweed. Anyway the sight'll be soon leavin' me.'

'Them that talk about dyin' are the longest to live . . . But here give me your eggs and less of this ould blether.'

She began unwrapping the few eggs; he always changed them for tea, sugar, or bread, and what with his pension coming to him every week, digging his own spuds, and fishing off the rocks, he was able to make a good living.

He delayed in the shop as long as he could, and only when the early dusk began to crush the light from the window did he make to go.

'The right ould miser,' the shopkeeper said to herself as he stooped out.

He blinked his eyes in the greyish light and joined the old men at the gable; they always spent their evenings arguing about ships that came ashore or about the place-names of their island. John Joe was the patriarch of the company and no one doubted his word. They all noticed something jaunty about Jamesy's step, the shrug of his shoulders, and the cock of his head. John Joe fidgeted and coughed loudly; what had Jamesy in his mind? What was he going to ask them?

'Comin' along the road I had the queerest thought,' he began slowly. They all held their pipes, waiting. 'I was thinkin' there's nothin' lastin' in this life except wan thing. D' any of yez know what that is?'

The three men looked perplexed at Jamesy, their slow-moving old brains seeking for an answer. John Joe spat out and tucked the tails of his muffler under his oxters. Jamesy grunted.

'D'ye know what it is? . . . I'll tell ye . . . it's stone that is lasting . . . Stone! Stone!' and he hammered out the words with his stick.

'How so?'

Like someone performing an ancient rite he slowly raised his stick; it trembled for a moment on the graveyard, and then slowly turned to Croc-na Screilean, a small hill gathering a skirt of darkness from the falling night.

'D'ye see Croc-na-Screilean,' he said, his voice quavering. 'Is there any change in it since we were childer? It hasn't changed, man, no more than the colour of the sea . . . why? . . . Because it's stone. Stone, the only lasting thing on this earth!'

They all stood silent; McDonnell and Johnny John Beg turned puzzled eyes to John Joe. John Joe took the pipe from his lips.

''Tisn't the hill that is lasting, but the memories that belong to it,' he said, pointing the shank of his pipe at Jamesy.

'That's the truth you're sayin',' put in McDonnell.

'It's the hill that's lasting, because it's stone,' Jamesy stamped back.

John Joe's mind was working quickly.

'A hill is only a hill if it has no memories; it has no life!' And then in excitement he raised his voice : 'I declare to God when I look at Croc-na-Screilean tisn't a hill I see at all, but our people—the McDonnells, the McCurdys, and McQuilkins, and the rest—fightin' the invaders in the hollow, and our women and children screamin' and shoutin' at them from the hill. 'Tis that what the hill means to me.'

'Aren't all them people dead and gone and the hill's the same,' Jamesy answered.

'They're not dead!' they shouted at him in chorus.

'Aren't their children's children here still? Aren't we the same stock?' added Johnny John Beg.

'And where'd we all be if our people hadn't married and made life. Where'd the island be? It'd be a rocky desert, a place for rabbits and wild birds and no one left to talk about Croc-na-Screilean and the stories that belong to it; it'd be only a hill—a dead hill!'

'And when you're dead yourself, Jamesy, you're dead for ever with no child to bear your name.'

They all added taunts about his childless life. He laughed at them.

'Where will yez all be in a number of years? Yez'll all be dead and rotten and forgotten and Croc-na-Screilean will be there without a change.' His eyes travelled to the graveyard : 'Stone is lasting! The name of Heaney will last!' With this he left them, his dog jumping up at him, glad to be on the road again.

'He's daft,' said John Joe, looking after him. 'Crazy! That's what living alone has done for him. And his slutthery old sod of a house that even a swallow would turn up its nose at.'

Jamesy laughed as he trudged away from them, his mind aflame with the vision of the headstone.

'Dead!' he said aloud to himself. 'Dead! Little do they know!'

The blue of the sky was darkening and a few stars were coming out. Behind him the oil-lamps in the village were turning the windows to gold and doors were being shut against the chill air. The road was blackening. The frost had thawed on the scraggy bushes and drops of water had formed on the bleak thorns. His step rang sharp on the road. The goat bleated and came to meet him, rubbing her teeth against his side.

Once back in the house he locked the door, hooked the blind to the window, and took a box from the roof-tree. By the light of a candle he looked at his money, his pension money, that he had saved for years. Next week he'd take it all to the mainland and arrange about the headstone.

He brewed more tea for himself, cut big slices off the loaf, and bruised a fresh slice for the collie. He was happy. He stretched out a hand and patted the dog. Smoke blew down the chimney and smarted his eyes.

In bed he lay awake looking through the window at the star-sprinkled sky with its rags of cloud skimming past the moon. The cross-sash of the window cast its blurred shadow on the bed. The old man's mind rehearsed the proposed visit to the stonecutter's, and when the first blast of an approaching storm ploofed on the roof like a bed-tick he curled himself in the blankets. He dozed for awhile but the rising wind and his excited mind kept sleep away from him.

His rusty bait-can scringed against the wall outside and then he heard it being lifted from its nail and sent clattering across the street. The wind continued to rise; it raked and roared in the tree at the gable and swished across the thatch like a mighty wave. The roar of it made him cower in his bed and the loud grumbles of it in the chimney set the dog barking. Jamesy shouted to her to lie down, but she continued to bark as the wind dunted against the walls and made them shake. Fear seized Jamesy; he felt as if the scraw of a roof would be lifted from off his head. He got out of bed and stood on a chair to get his box. The wind whistled sharply in the slits of the door and groped under the threshold. Wisps of cold air whirled around him. He put the box under the bed and let the dog into the room.

The crackling of sticks made him turn to the window and by the light of the moon he saw his hens fluttering wildly from the streaming wreck of the shed. He clutched at his beads; if he should did before he had the arrangements made for his Stone! He trembled; but the leaping thoughts of his headstone, sparking and burning in his brain, took his mind from the prayers. He'd wait no longer; next boat-day he'd be off to the mainland.

The sea rose with the wind; the thundering waves pounded the rocks and the spray speckled the window. His thorn tree bent to the flood of the storm like an old woman with flying hair. The straw of his hen-shed was swirled high by the wind.

Another crash made Jamesy sit upright. His mouth hung open with fear. He found himself looking at the moon through the branches of a tree. His tree was down! Its bare twigs scraped the window. A cold sweat broke out on him; it was safer to stay inside; he covered his head with the clothes.

As the night advanced the storm broke into intermittent gusts and by dawn it had blown itself out, and Jamesy, exhausted lay in a deep sleep, the collie curled up beside him. It was the dog, licking his brow, that wakened him to the morning. It was clear and cold, filled with the noise of the sea. The land was scoured clean, but around the cottage the storm had played itself.

When he opened the door the scene saddened him. The wreckage of the shed was strewn up on the hill; the street littered with straw and twigs, the thatch combed to one side like the grass on a flooded river-bank. He looked at the tree lying on the ground, its bony roots clawing the air. Life the tree had, and now it is dead : stone has no life, but it lives! He'd have something for John Joe this evening.

All day he chopped at the branches of the tree and hammered the remnants of the shed together. It was useless to build a shed of timber; stone's the thing, he said to himself. From a hill near the house he dug up the scraws that patched the rocks, the dead heather roots tearing dryly under the spade. He built them around the bottom of the shed and all the while the goat lay at the gable chewing unconcernedly, the hens bunched around her.

In the early evening he struck off for the village with his dog. He was contented with himself and the work he had done. His mind clung to the things he had ready for his three companions; the strong ash hurled to the ground; the wooden-shed; and the withered heather clinging for life to the barren rocks. From the crest on the road his house, bare of the outspreading arms of the tree, looked desolate. Looking at it Jamesy became sad and regretful; awakened memories of the tree's companionship arose within him and made him linger on the hill. But the shouts of playing children came to him faintly on the calm chill air and he grinned to himself cunningly and strode off towards the village.

Outside the graveyard on the hill he halted. Slyly he walked to the gate and entered. And then his eyes bulged and he stiffened with awe. He looked for the McBride stone; it was gone; a great vacancy held the sky. The monument lay in fragments on the top of the grave and crosses were tilted or blown down.

Slowly Jamesy backed away. His eyes stared at the great carnage of stone. He left the gate open and made off for home again. The dog stood sideways on the top of the hill, waiting for him to turn, but he went on and on, going quickly, afraid to look back, while behind him the children screamed in delight as they gathered the sticks washed up on the stormy shore.

Steeplejacks

The brickworks at the edge of the town had been closed down for many years and wind and rain had made wrecks of the old kilns and drying sheds. Nearby in the deep pit lay a pond of greenish water and across it on sunny days there stretched the shadow of the tall brick chimney with its lightning-conductor, a chimney that was a landmark for miles around.

One day it was rumoured that the brickworks was to be reopened and the rumour became a fact when Tim Rooney, a famous steeplejack, arrived one morning with three assistants to repoint and renovate the tall chimney. After much manoeuvring and hammering the sectional ladder was placed upright against the face of the chimney, and from the top of it Tim gazed down at his three workmates who were shading their eyes against the sun and staring up at him. From the broad lip of the chimney he hauled out abandoned jackdaws' nests and flung the bundles of sticks into the air, and after putting his hammers in a straw basket that was suspended from a pulley-block he plucked at the rope and signalled to his men to lower away. He watched the basket move to the ground in short, irregular jerks, and before descending the ladder himself he looked across the fields to the houses at the edge of the town where smoke rose untroubled from the chimney pots and freshly washed shirts hung limp from the lines in the backyards. The sight of the clothes made him thirsty and he licked his dry lips and resting his hands on the topmost rung of the ladder, now warm under the sun, he began to descend with slow and definite rhythm.

'Well,' he said on reaching the ground and clapping the red dust from his hands, 'there's a grand view from the top. Three counties lie below you,' he exaggerated, 'and you can gaze down the throats of all the chimney pots in the streets beyond. Well, John,' he addressed the youngest of the group, a lad of 18, 'what about that jaunt you're to make to the top? When you're married you'll be able to boast to your children how you climbed to the top of the tallest chimney in the town.'

John's gaze travelled slowly to the top of the chimney but he didn't move or speak.

'He boasted all week he'd climb it,' said George, the eldest of the group.

'Nobody's forcing him if he doesn't want to go,' Tim declared, unwilling to encourage him. 'We'll take our lunch first.'

'I'm not afraid,' John answered and spat on his hands. 'It'd be better if I'd climb on a fasting stomach. I'll go before we take our lunch.'

'It would be better for us all if you would,' George mocked. 'You'll be seasick before you're halfway up.'

'I was never seasick in my life.'

'Hard for you! The biggest boat you were ever in was a swing-boat in the children's playground.'

'Here goes!' John answered, fastened his belt and cart-wheeled towards the base of the chimney. He gripped the side of the ladder with one hand, bowed gracefully, and said, 'You're now about to witness an exhibition of how a chimney should be climbed. There's nothing in it, gentlemen, as long as you keep your head. Nothing in it.'

'Hear! Hear!' George applauded and eyed him humorously. Tim said nothing.

The lad climbed some rungs rapidly and then with slow caution ascended another four. His toe dislodged a piece of mortar and he heard it clink against the ladder on its way to the ground. He paused, frightened. Above him he saw the ladder converge at the top like railway lines. He had a long way to go yet, and on looking down to measure his distance from the ground he saw, in one swaying moment, the old drying sheds buckle and stretch like an accordion. He held grimly to the ladder and allowed his head to clear. Sweat oozed in blobs on his forehead and his hands became clammy. In front of him he saw tiny hairs of moss growing like moles between the bricks and he noticed with rising terror that some of the bricks were cracked. He closed his eyes, swallowed with difficulty, and made an attempt to descend. His foot missed the lower rung and his trouser-leg caught on it and rolled back, and for a moment he felt the free air on his bare leg. He drew his two feet together, twined his arms round a rung of the ladder and remained still.

A tizzing sound trembled through the sides of the ladder. They were hammering on it, signalling to him to come down. He was afraid to move or to look up or look down. He heard Tim call up to him, but what advice was given he couldn't make out. The gray rope at the side of the ladder tautened and presently the basket halted beside him, but when he put a hand on it it swung away from him and in an instant he gripped the rung above his head and closed his eyes to shut out the drunken tilting of the chimney.

'Hold tightly, John, like a good lad,' Tim shouted, his voice near at hand. 'Hold tightly and don't look down.'

Tim was now directly below him : 'Don't be afeared,' he was saying, 'give me your right foot. Let it loose and I'll guide it. That's the stuff. Now give me the left foot. Hold tight with your hands and leave the feet to me . . . Here we go again. Put the right foot down and now the left beside it. That's the way it's done. That's the ticket! We'll make a steeplejack out of you yet, never fear. Off we go again. First the right and now the left.'

'Are we nearly there?' John asked without turning his head.

'We haven't far to go. Keep looking up and you'll be safe in port before you know where you are.'

Tim hurried down the last few rungs; John followed him and on reaching the ground his workmates clapped loudly.

'It's not as easy as it looks,' he breathed, his face a green colour and his eyes large with fright. 'Was I up far?'

'You were near the top.'

'I was like hell.'

'I warned you you'd be seasick but you wouldn't heed me.'

'Give over,' Tim said. 'We all have to learn. For a first attempt he didn't do badly.'

'Never again,' John said and sat on the ground which swayed like the deck of a ship.

Tim patted him on the shoulder : 'Breathe in the air deeply and you'll be as right as rain in no time.'

They helped him to his feet and gave him a drink of water from a can that lay in the long grass out of the sun. They spread newspapers in the cool shade of the hedge, opened their lunchboxes, and took out their thermos flasks. In front of them across the sunny field the windows of the houses were all open and the smoke from the chimneys lay in a smother above the roofs.

'It's so still here,' Tim said, 'it'd be a nice place for a cemetery. But you'll not be going there for a while yet, John.'

John smiled like a convalescent and his hand trembled as he took the cup of tea that Tim poured out for him. He drank it slowly, and when he had finished he lay back on the grass and felt his nausea slip away from him. For awhile he listened to the men talking, and then closing his eyes he tried to relax. He dozed over, but the smell from the men's pipes made him feel sickish and he sat up and rubbed his forehead. Above the hedge towered the chimney and as he stared at it he saw a young boy halfway up the ladder.

'Tim, look!' and he turned pale and felt his head grow light.

Tim peered through the leaves in the hedge and saw the boy nearing the top of the chimney.

'For the love of God, men, don't budge, don't breathe,' he ordered. 'There's a young lad at the top of the ladder. Keep still and don't frighten him.'

The two men turned and watched the boy lever himself on to the lip of the chimney and sit dangling his legs as if he were seated on a roadside wall.

'We mustn't show ourselves,' Tim urged, 'mustn't let him know we see him. If he has the head to climb up, he'll have the head to get down.'

Suddenly the boy ceased dangling his legs and crawled on his knees round the lip of the chimney. He did the complete circle and on reaching the top of the ladder he turned his back to descend. He twined his arms round the topmost rung and clung to it without moving. The men watched and waited, bending the branches of the hedge to see better.

'He's staying there because he can't get down,' John said. 'I know what it's like—he's afraid to move. We must do something. Tim. Go up after him; help him the way you helped me.'

'Take it cool; that boy will get down all right. I know what I'm talking about.'

'He's stuck. He's afraid to move—anyone can see that! I'm going for the fire brigade; they'll get him down,' John said, springing to his feet.

'Don't make a fool of yourself. Stay where you are. That boy has a head for heights, I tell you. He'll manage by himself if we leave him alone and not startle him.'

The boy still clung to the top rung, but made no attempt to descend.

'I can't bear to look at him any longer,' John said, and before his workmates could stop him he was running along the hedge to the town.

At that moment, slowly and steadily, the boy began to descend, sometimes halting to look around him.

'That's the way, my boy,' Tim breathed to himself, 'that's the way to do it. But for the love of God, don't look down. Come on, another rung. You're just half way. Come on, what are you hesitating for!'

From their look-out behind the hedge they watched intently every movement that he made. They saw him halt, rub each hand in turn on his jersey, look up, and once more begin to ascend.

'Did you ever see the like of that for cheek since God made you? There's the makings of a great steeplejack in that boy,' George said.

'He has the head all right, but I wish I had my hands on him before John fetches the fire brigade,' Tim said. 'I should have left someone on watch when we were at our lunch.'

The boy had now reached the top of the ladder and after struggling onto the lip of the chimney he stood up on it, walked round to the lightning-conductor and gripped it like a Roman soldier with his spear. At that moment a woman came out of the end house across the fields and taking damp clothes from her washing basket she hung them on the line. Then, shading her eyes, she called to left and right : 'Jackie, Jackie, Jackie.' She didn't see him crouched at the top of the chimney, and when she had gone back to the house he descended the ladder rapidly and raced across the fields.

'Thanks be to God he's safe anyway,' Tim said and rose to his feet. 'Never again will I leave the ladder without a watchman.'

He walked across the field to the end house and on reaching the open door he called to the woman as she moved about the dark kitchen and asked if he could have a word with her son.

'I hope he hasn't been up to any mischief, Mister,' she said, coming to the door.

'Nothing much. I was wondering if you'd like him to be a steeplejack.'

'A steeplejack! What on earth's that?'

'My job—pointing and renovating mill chimneys.'

The woman smiled : 'Is it our Jackie! He hasn't the heart of a rabbit, Mister, and that's the truth.'

'I can tell you he climbed to the top of the brickyard chimney when we'd our backs turned.

'He wouldn't do the like of that, Mister!' she said and stared at him incredulously.

'He did, indeed. Ask him yourself.'

She beckoned Jackie beside her and scrutinized the red dust on his jersey and trousers.

'Where were you?' she shouted and gripped his shoulder.

'Over in the brickfields, Mother.'

'What were you doing?'

'Looking around and playing.'

'Playing at what?'

Jackie lowered his head but didn't answer.

'You climbed the ladder to the top of the chimney,' Tim challenged him.

'Speak up to the man, Jackie, where's your manners!'

Jackie plucked at a loose thread on his jersey.

'You walked round the lip of the chimney and put your hand on the lightning conductor,' Tim pressed.

'Merciful God!' the mother exclaimed and sat down on

a chair. 'Wait till I get my breath back. My boyo, but you're a heartscald. You'd some poor body's blessing about you when you weren't killed stone dead.'

'He has a head for heights. You should let him follow his gift. He's a born climber, a born steeplejack.'

'He'll not be able to climb into bed when I'm done with him . . . And wait till his father hears about it . . . It's the last chimney he'll climb in this life . . . Oh, you'll be in you good safe school tomorrow if you're fit to go . . . I'm thankful to you, Mister, for if I'd seen him at the top of the chimney the sight'd never leave my eyes.'

The bell of the fire brigade could be heard approaching the edge of the town.

'I'll have to go,' Tim said. 'But when the lad's the age keep my job in mind for him. There's good money in it.'

He hurriedly took his leave and headed across the field to the hedge where his two workmates awaited him.

Evening in Winter

Charley was six at the time, or maybe seven. His Mammie was beside him in a white apron, her hands on her lap doing nothing. His Daddy lay stretched in sleep on the sofa. Sunday evening was always quiet. The fire-glow filled the room. It glowed redly on Charley's knees and face, glinted on the fender, and threw shadows on the ceiling and the red-tiled floor. It was nice to be sitting alone with your Daddy and Mammie, feeling the heat on your knees, and listening to the kettle singing, and ashes falling in the grate. In the fire you could see animals and sometimes men and sometimes ships, and when your eyes got sticky you could just sit and look at nothing.

Suddenly the milkman knocked and Charley jumped. His Mammie went into the scullery for the white jug. His Daddy wakened and took out his big watch in the fireglow.

'Boys-o-boys!' he said. 'Is it that time?'

He got up and was on his feet when Mammie came back and placed the jug on the clean table. Daddy was very tall standing on the floor, with the fire winking on his watch-chain and his face all red and rosy.

'Do you think you'll go this evening?' Mammie said.

'Indeed I will,' said Daddy.

'Maybe you'd take Charley with you, he never gets anywhere.'

So Charley was going out with his Daddy, out at night

when the lamps would be lit and all other wee boys in bed.

His mother put on his little round hat with the elastic that nipped him under the chin, and when he was going out the front door she stooped and kissed him.

'Say a prayer for your Mammie who has to stay at home,' she said.

And now they were walking down the street. He felt big to be out so late with the sky dark and the lamps lit. The snow had fallen. It wasn't deep snow, but it covered the ground, and lines of it lay on the black garden railings, and on the arms of the lamp-posts. The milkman's cart was near a lamp and its brass fittings shone and steam came from the horse's nose. The milkman said to his Daddy, 'a cold evening that,' and steam came from his mouth, too. Then his cans rattled. The cart moved on in front and the wheels began to unwind black ribbons on the snow.

They walked out of the street on to the road, on to the road where the trams ran. Charley put his hand in his Daddy's pocket and it was lovely and warm. Up in the sky it was black, as black as ink, and far away was the moon which Mammie called God's lamp, and stars were round it like little candle lights.

A tram passed, groaning up the hill where they were walking. Sparks, green ones and red ones and blue ones, crackled from the trolley, but the tram went on and slithered out of sight. And now there was nothing on the road only the snow and the black lines where the trams ran. Up above were the telephone wires covered with crumbs of snow, but the trolley wires were all dark. Presently they lit up with gold light and soon a black motor-car came slushing down the hill, covered with snow. Then it was very quiet.

Other people, big people all in black, were out and most of them were walking in the same direction as

Charley and his Daddy. They passed shops, the sweet-shop with Mrs. Dempsey standing at the door.

'Good-night, Mister Conor,' she said. His Daddy raised his hat, the hard hat that he wore on Sundays.

'Do you know Missus Dempsey, Daddy?'

'I do, son.'

'I know her; that's where I buy when I've pennies.' But his Daddy looked in front with the steam coming out of his mouth.

They passed policemen standing in doorways, stamping their feet, the policemen who chased you for playing football in the streets. But Charley wasn't afraid now, he was walking with his hand clutched tightly in his Daddy's—inside the big warm pocket.

After a while they came to the chapel. All the people seemed to be going to the chapel. It was dark outside, but a man stood in a lighted porch holding a wooden plate, and on the plate Charley's father put pennies.

Inside it was warm and bright. You could smell the heat as you walked up the aisle. His Daddy's boots squeaked and that was a sign they weren't paid for. They went into a seat up near the altar and his father knelt down with a white handkerchief spread under his knees. Charley sat with his legs swinging to and fro. At the sides were windows, and when tram-cars passed you could see lightning and blue diamonds and red diamonds.

Someone came in at the end of their seat and Charley and his Daddy had to move up. It wasn't nice for people to move you into a cold place, when you had the seat warmed.

A priest came out. Charley could answer the prayers like the rest and he felt very big. After a long time they stood up to sing and Charley turned round to look at the organ-man away high up at the back of the church. The organ looked like big, hot-pipes. At the end of the hymn he said :

'Are we going home now, Daddy?'

'S-s-sh,' his Daddy said softly.

'Well, when are we going home ?'

His Daddy didn't answer. Charley lifted the little round hat and began crackling the elastic and putting it in his mouth. His Daddy told him to sit at peace.

A priest came into the pulpit. He talked about lightning, and he said that the sun would be dark, and that the stars would fall from Heaven. He talked for a long, long time, but Charley fell asleep. After a while his father caught him by the arm and with difficulty he opened his eyes. A big boy with a long taper was lighting rows of candles and Charley began to count them. One candle didn't light at first, and he had to come back and touch it a few times. Soon the altar was all lit up and here and there were bunches of flowers. Dim lights shone from the brass bell that stood on the altar steps like a big gold mushroom.

The organ began playing softly, very softly, and Charley turned to see what was wrong. A woman in the seat behind him was praying, her lips moving in a low whistle. He watched the moving lips and then they stopped suddenly. The woman was making a face at him and he turned and sat closer to his Daddy.

He filled his mind with everything, everything to tell his big brothers and sisters. There were boys with fat brass candlesticks and a priest with a golden clock that sparkled with lights. God was on the altar, too, behind a little glass window with gold spikes all around it. A boy was shaking a silver thing like a lamp and smoke came out of it, nice-smelling smoke, and if you shut your eyes it made a noise like nails in a tin.

The organ began to growl and people to sing. Charley put his fingers to the flaps of his ears. You could hear the noise very small, then it would get big like thunder, and if you moved your fingers in and out the noise would go ziz-zaz and a ah-aha-aaah! But it soon stopped. People bowed their heads and Daddy bowed his head too. Charley covered his eyes with his hands, but looked through his fingers to see what was going on. Someone coughed far, far away. Someone else coughed. Then it became so still you could hear your heart thumping.

The bell on the altar rang once. His Daddy whispered something to himself, and when the bell rang again Charley heard him say, 'My Lord and my God!' He thought of his Mammie and he told God to love his Mammie who had to stay at home. He closed his eyes and he saw her in a snowy apron, the white jug on the table and he wondered if she would have cake for his tea, cake with currants in it.

And now they were going home, out into the cold air, and on to the road where the trams ran.

His big brothers and sisters were in when he got home. They were taking tea and there was cake with currants in it on the table. They asked him questions, but laughed at his answers, so he just sat and ate his cake. But his Mammie was good and he told her that when the bell rang Daddy said, 'My Lord and my God!' But his Daddy didn't laugh at this. He just said, 'That child is dying with sleep, he should be in bed.'

So his Mammie brought him to bed, up to the bedroom where the red-lamp was, the red-lamp that burned like a tulip's head before a picture of Holy God. He knelt and said his prayers on the cold, oilcloth floor. In bed it was cold, too, colder than the seat in the chapel. But it soon got warm; and he thought of the organ in his ears . . . the candle that wouldn't light . . . the tram that went up the hill with lights crackling from the trolley . . . and stars falling . . . falling . . .

The White Mare

'What about Paddy, Kate? He'll be raging if we let him lie any longer and it such a brave morning.'

'Och, let him rage away, Martha. He'll know his driver before night if he ploughs the field.'

''Deed that's the truth, and with an old mare that's done and dropping off her feet.'

'He'll get sense when it's too late. And to hear him gabbling you'd think he was a young man and not the spent old thorn that he is. But what's the use of talking! Give him a call.'

Kate, seated on a stool, blew at the fire with the bellows, blew until the flames were spurting madly in and out between the brown sods. Martha waited until the noise of the blazing fire had ceased, and then rapped loudly at the room door off the kitchen. The knocking was answered by a husky voice.

Paddy was awake, sitting up in the bed, scratching his head with his two hands and blinking at the bare window in the room. His face was bony and unshaven, his moustache grey and straggly. Presently he threw aside the blankets and crawled out backwards on to the cold cement floor. He stood at the window. In the early hours of the morning it had rained, but now it was clear. A high wind had combed the white hair of the sky, and on the bare thorn at the side of the byre shivered swollen buds of rain. Across the cobbled street was his stubble field, bounded on one side by a hedge and a hill, and on the other sides by loose stones. Two newly-ploughed furrows ran down the centre and at the top of them lay his plough with a crow swaying nervously on one of the handles. Last evening when the notion took him he had commenced the ploughing, and today, with the help of God, he'd finish it. He thought of the rough feel of the handles, the throb of the coulter cutting the clay, and the warm sweaty smell from his labouring mare.

With difficulty he stretched himself to his full height, his bony joints creaking, and his lungs filling with the rain-washed air that came through the open window; he drew in great breaths of it, savouring it as he would savour the water from a spring well. As he was about to turn away, the crow rose up suddenly and flew off. At that moment Kate was crossing to the byre, one hand holding a can, and the other a stick. Paddy watched, trying to guess from her movements the kind of temper she was in this morning. But he noted nothing unusual about her. There was the same active walk, the black triangle of shawl dipping down her back, and the grey head with the man's cap on it. To look at her you wouldn't think she was drawing the pension for over six years. No, there wasn't another house in the whole island with three drawing the pension—not another house! We're a great stock and no mistake; a great pity none of us married!

Kate's voice pierced the air as she shouted at a contrary cow. Oh, a good kind woman, but a tartar when you stirred her. He'd hold his tongue this morning till he had the mare tackled and then they could barge away. Anyway what do women know about a man's job, with their milking cows, and feeding hens, and washing clothes? H'm! a field has to be ploughed and it takes a man to plough it.

When he came from the room Kate was just in from milking and Martha moved slowly about the table arranging the mugs and the farls of bread. Paddy stooped and took his clay-caked boots from below the table. He knew by the look of his sisters that he'd have to lace them himself this morning. It always caused him pain to stoop, but what matter, he'd soon be out in the quiet of the fields where no one would say a word to him.

They all sat at the table together, eating silently and with the slow deliberation that comes with the passing years. Now and again as Paddy softened his bread in the tea, Kate would give him a hard little look. It was coming, he knew it. If only they'd keep silent until he had finished. But it was coming; the air was heavy with stifled talk.

'I suppose you'll do half the field today,' began Kate.

''Deed and I'll do it all,' he replied with a touch of hardness in his voice knowing he must be firm.

'Now, Paddy, you should get Jamesy's boys over to help you,' said Martha pleadingly.

'Them wee buttons of men! I'd have it done while they'd be thinkin' about it. I wouldn't have them about the place again, with their ordering this and ordering that, and their tea after their dinner, and wanting their pipes filled every minute with good tobacco. I can do it all myself with the help of God. All myself!' and with this he brought his mug down sharply on the table.

'If you get another attack of the pains it's us'll have to suffer,' put in Kate, 'attending you morning, noon and night. Have you lost your wits, man! It's too old you're getting and it'd be better if we sold the mare and let the two bits of fields.'

Paddy kept silent; it was better to let them fire away.

'The mare's past her day,' Kate continued. 'It's rest the poor thing wants an' not pulling a plough with a done man behind it.'

'Done, is it? There's work in me yet, and I can turn a furrow as straight as anyone in the island. Done! H'm I've my work to be doing.'

He got up, threw his coat across his shoulder, and strode towards the door. His two sisters watched him go out, nodding their heads. 'Ah, but that's a foolish, hard-headed man. There's no fool like an old fool!'

Paddy crossed to the stable and the mare nickered when she heard his foot on the cobbled street. Warm, hay-scented air met him as he opened the door. Against the wall stood the white mare. She cocked her ears and turned her head towards the light. She was big and fat with veins criss-crossing on her legs like dead ivy roots on the limbs of a tree. Her eyes were wet-shining and black, their upper lids fringed with long grey lashes. Paddy stroked her neck and ran his fingers through her yellow-grey mane.

A collar with the straw sticking out of it was soon buckled on, and with chains rattling from her sides he led her through the stone-slap into the field. He looked at the sky, at the sea with its patches of mist, and then smilingly went to his plough. Last evening the coulter was cutting too deep and he now adjusted it, giving it a final smack with the spanner that rang out clear in the morning air. The mare was sniffing the rain-wet grass under the hedge and she raised her head jerkily as he approached, sending a shower of cold drops from the bushes down his neck. He shivered, but spoke kindly to the beast as he led her to be tackled. In a few minutes all was ready, and gripping the handles in God's name, he ordered the horse forward, and his day's work began.

The two sisters eyed him from the window. His back was towards them. Above the small stone fence they could see his bent fingers, his navy-blue trousers with a brown patch on the seat of them, his grey shirt sleeves, the tattered back of his waistcoat, and above his shabby hat the swaying quarters of the mare.

'Did you ever see such a man since God made you! I declare to goodness he'll kill that mare,' said Martha.

'It's himself he'll kill if he's not careful. Let me bold Paddy be laid up after this and 'tis the last field he'll plough, for I'll sell the mare, done beast and all as she is!' replied Kate, pressing her face closer to the window.

Paddy was unaware of their talk. His eyes were on the sock as it slid slowly through the soft earth and pushed the gleaming furrows to the side. He was living his life. What call had he for help! Was it sit by and look at Jamesy's boys ploughing the field, and the plough wobbling to and fro like you'd think they were learning to ride a bicycle.

'Way up, girl,' he shouted to the mare, ''way up, Maggie!' and his veins swelled on his arms as he leant on the handles. The breeze blowing up from the sea, the cold smell of the broken clay, and the soft hizzing noise of the plough, all soothed his mind and stirred him to new life.

As the day advanced the sun rose higher, but there was little heat from it, and frosty vapours still lingered about the rockheads and about the sparse hills. But slowly over the little field horse and plough still moved, moved like timeless creatures of the earth, while alongside, their shadows followed on the clay. Overhead and behind swarmed the gulls, screeching and darting for the worms, their flitting shadows falling coolly on Paddy's neck and on the back of the mare. At the end of the ridge he stopped to take a rest, surveying with pleasure the number of turned furrows, and wondering if his sisters were proud of him now. He looked up at the house : it was low and whitewashed, one end thatched and the other corrugated. There seemed to be no life about in except the smoke from the chimney and a crow plucking at the thatch. Soon it flew off with a few straws hanging from its bill. It's a pity he hadn't the gun now, he'd soon stop that thief; at nesting-time they wouldn't leave a roof above your head. But tomorrow he'd fix them. He spat on his hands and gripped the handles.

At two o'clock he saw Kate making down at the top of the field and he moved to the hedge. She brought him a few empty sacks to sit on; a good kind girl when you took her the right way. She had the real stuff in the eggpunch, too, nothing like it for a working man.

When he had taken his first swig of tea she said quietly, 'It's time you were quitting, Paddy.'

He must be careful. 'Did you see that devil of a crow on the thatch?'

'I didn't, thank God. But I've heard it said that it's the sure sign of a death.'

'Did you now?' he replied with a smile. 'Isn't that queer, and me always thinking that it was the sign of new life and them nesting?'

It's no use trying to frighten him, she thought, no use talking to him; he'll learn his own lesson before morning. Up she got and went off.

'Give the mare a handful of hay and a bucket of water,' he called after her.

He lay back, smoking his pipe at his ease, enjoying the look of the ribbed field and the familiar scene. To his right over the stone fence lay the bony rocks stretching their lanky legs into the sea; and now and again he could hear the hard rattle of the pebbles being sucked into the gullet of the waves. Opposite on a jutting headland rose the white column of the East Lighthouse, as lonely-looking as ever. There never was much stir on this side of the island anyway. It was a mile or more from the quay where the little sailing boats went twice a week to Ballycastle. But what little there was of land was good. As he looked down at the moist clay, pressing nail-marks in it with his toe, he pitied the people in the Lower End with their shingly fields and stunted crops. How the news would travel to them tonight about his ploughing! Every mouthful of talk would be about him and the old white mare. He puffed at his pipe vigorously and a sweet smile came over his wrinkled face. Then the shouts of the children coming from school made him aware of the passing time.

He must get up now for the sun would set early. He knocked out his pipe on the heel of his boot. When he made to rise he felt stiff in the shoulders, and a needle of pain jagged one of his legs making him give a silly little laugh. It's a bad thing to sit too long and the day flying. He walked awkwardly over to Maggie, and presently they were going slowly over the field again. The yellow-green bands at each side of the dark clay grew narrower and narrower as each new furrow was turned. Soon they would disappear. The sky was clear and the sun falling; the daylight might hold till he had finished.

The coulter crunched on a piece of delph and its white chips were mosaiced on the clay. 'Man alive, but them's the careless women,' he said aloud. 'If the mare cut her feet there'd be a quare how-d'ye-do!' At that moment Kate came out to the stone fence and gathered clothes that had been drying. She stood with one hand on her cheek, looking at the slow, almost imperceptible, movement of the plough. She turned, shooshed the hens from her feet, and went in slamming the door behind her.

Over the rock heads the sun was setting, flushing the clay with gold, and burnishing the mould-board and the buckles on the horse. Two more furrows and the work was done. He paused for a rest, and straightened himself with difficulty. His back ached and his head throbbed, but what he saw was soothing. On the side of a hill his three sheep were haloed in gold and their long shadows sloped away from them. It was a grand sight, praise be to God, a grand sight! He bent to the plough again, his legs feeling thick and heavy. 'Go on, Maggie!' he ordered. 'Two more furrows and we're done.'

The words whipped him to a new effort and he became light with excitement. One by one the gulls flew off and the western sky burned red. A cold breeze sharp with the smell of salt breathed in the furrows. And then he was finished; the furrows as straight as loom-threads and not a bit of ground missed. A great piece of work, thanks be to God; a great bit of work for an old man and an old mare. He put on his coat and unyoked her. She felt light and airy as he led her by the head across the cobbles. Gently he took the collar from her, the hot vapour rising into the chilled air, and with a dry sack wiped her sides and legs and neck. A great worker; none better in the whole island. He stroked her between the ears and smiled at the way she coaxingly tossed her head. He put her in the stable; later on he'd be back with a bucket of warm mash.

It was semi-dark when he turned his back on the stable and saw the orange rectangle of light in the kitchen window. It was cold, and he shivered and shrugged his shoulders as he stood listening at the door.

In the kitchen it was warm and bright. The turf was piled high, and Martha and Kate sat on opposite sides of the hearth, Kate knitting and Martha peeling potatoes. He drew a chair to the fire and sat down between them in silence. The needles clicked rapidly, and now and then a potato plopped into the bucket. He must get out his pipe; a nice way to receive a man after a day's ploughing. The needles stopped clicking and Kate put her hands on her lap and stared at him from behind her silver-rimmed spectacles. Paddy took no notice as he went slowly on cutting his plug and grinding it between his palms. Then he spat in the fire, and Kate retorted by prodding the sods with her toe, sending sparks up the chimney. The spit hissed in the strained silence. The kettle sang and he rose to feed the mare.

'Just leave that kettle alone, Mister MacNeil,' said Martha.

'The mare has to be fed!'

'It's little you care about the poor dumb beast, and you out killing yourself and her, when it would suit you better to be in peeling these spuds.'

'It's little you do in the house but make a few bits of meals, and it's time you were stirring yourself and getting a hard-worked man a good supper.'

'If you're hard-worked, who's to blame, I ask you?' flared Kate.

He was done for now. He could always manage Martha; if he raised his voice it was the end of her. But Kate—he feared her though he wouldn't admit it to himself.

'Do you hear me, Paddy MacNeil? Who's to blame? Time and again we have told you to let the fields and have sense. But no; me bold boy must be up and leppin' about like a wild thing. And what'll the women in the island be talking about, I ask you? Ah! well we know what they'll be saying. "It's a shame that Paddy MacNeil's mean old sisters wouldn't hire a man to work the land. There they have poor Paddy and his seventy years, out in the cold of March ploughing with the old white mare. And the three of them getting the pension. I always knew there was a mean streak in them MacNeils." That's what they'll be saying, well we know it!'

'Talk sense, Kate, talk sense. Don't I know what they'll be saying. They'll be putting me up as an example to all and sundry. And . . .'

'But mark my words,' interrupted Kate, shaking a needle at him, 'if you're laid up after this you can attend to your pains yourself. I'm sick, sore and tired plastering and rubbing your shoulder and dancing attendance on you, and God knows I'm not able. I'm a done old woman myself, slaving from morning to night and little thanks I get for it.' Her voice quavered; crying she'll be next. It was best to keep silent.

'Get him his supper, Martha, till we get to bed—

another day like this and I'm fit for nothing.' She lifted her hands from her lap and the needles clicked slowly, listlessly.

In silence he took his supper. He was getting tired of these rows. When he had finished he went out with a bucket of warm mash for the mare. He felt very weary and sleepy, but the cold night braced him a little. The moon was up and the cobbles shone blue-white like the scales of a salmon. Maggie stirred when she heard the rasping handle of the bucket.

He closed the half-door of the stable, lit the candle, and sat on an upturned tub to watch the mare feeding. It was very still and she fed noisily, lifting her head now and again, the bran dripping from her mouth. Above the top of the door he could see the night-sky, the corrugated roof of the house, and the ash tree with its bare twigs shining in the moon. A little breeze blew its wavering pattern on the roof, and looking at it he thought of the gulls on the clay and the cool rush of their wings above his head. He shivered, and got up and closed the top half of the door. It was very still now; the mare had stopped feeding, her tail swished gently, and the warm hay glowed in the candlelight. There was great peace and comfort here. Under the closed door stole the night-wind, the bits of straw around the threshold rising gently and falling back again. A mouse came out from under the manger, rustled towards the bucket blinking its little eyes at the creature on the tub. Paddy squirted a spit at it and smiled at the way it raced off. He looked at the mare, watching slight tremors passing down her limbs. He got up, stroked her silky neck and scratched her between the ears. Then he gave her fresh hay and went out.

It was very peaceful with the moon shining on the fields and the sea. He wondered if his sisters were in bed. He hesitated at the stone fence looking at the cold darkness of the field and the bits of broken crockery catching the moonlight. Through the night there came to him clear and distinct the throb, throb of a ship's engine far out at sea. He held his breath to listen to it and then he saw its two unsteady mastlights, rounding the headland and moving like stars through the darkness. It made him sad to look at it and he sighed as he turned towards the house. He sniffed the air like a spaniel; there'd be rain before long; it would do a world of good now that the field was ploughed.

His sisters were in bed; the lamp was lowered and the ashes stirred. He quenched the lamp and went up to his room. The moonlight shone in the window so he needn't bother with a candle. He knelt on a chair to say his prayers; he'd make them short tonight, for he was tired, very tired. But his people couldn't be left out. The prayers came slowly. His mind wandered. The golden shaft of the lighthouse swept into the room, mysteriously and quietly—light—dark—light—dark. For years he had watched that light, and years after when he'd be dead and gone it would still flash, and there'd be no son or daughter to say a prayer for him. It's a stupid thing for a man not to get married and have children to pray for him; a stupid thing indeed! It was strange to be associating death with a lighthouse in the night, but in some way that thought had come to him now that he was old, and he knew that it would always come. He didn't stop to examine it. He got up and sat on the chair, fumbling at his coat.

He climbed into bed, the straw mattress rustling with his weight. He lay thinking of his day's work, waiting for sleep to fall upon him. He closed his eyes, but somehow sleep wouldn't come. The tiredness was wearing off him. He'd smoke for awhile, that would ease his mind. He was thinking too much; thinking kills sleep. The moonlight left the room and it became coldly dark. He stretched out his hand, groping for his pipe and matches. The effort shot a pain through his legs and he stifled a groan. At the other side of the wooden partition Kate and Martha heard him, but didn't speak. They lay listening to his movements. Then they heard the rasp of the match on the emery, heard him puffing at the pipe, and saw in their minds its warm glow in the cold darkness. There would be a long interval of silence, then the creak of his bed, and another muffled groan.

'Do you hear him?' whispered Kate. 'We're going to have another time of it with him. He has himself killed. But this is the last of it!'

'He'll be harrowing the field next,' said Martha.

'Harrow he will not. Tomorrow, send a note to the horse-dealer in Ballycastle.'

'Are you going to sell the mare, Kate?' Martha asked incredulously.

'Indeed I am. There's no sense left in that man's head while she's about.'

'Will you tell Paddy?'

'I'll tell him when she's sold, and that's time enough. So off with the note first thing in the morning.'

A handful of rain scattered itself on the tin roof above their heads. For awhile there was silence—deep and dark and listening. Then with a tree-like swish the rain fell, fell without ceasing, filling the room with cold streaks of noise.

Paddy lay listening to its hard pattering. He thought of the broken field soaking in the rain, and the disturbed creatures seeking shelter under the sod, rushing about with weakly legs clambering for a new home, while down in the sea the fish would be hiding in its brown tangled lair disturbed by no plough. It's strange the difference between the creatures; all the strange work of God, the God that knows all. Louder and louder fell the rain. 'It's well the mare's in that night,' he said to himself, 'and it's well the field's ploughed.' He pictured the sheep pressing into the wet rocks for shelter, and the rabbits scuttling to their holes. Then he wondered if he had closed the stable door; it was foolish to think that way; he closed it, of course he closed it. His thoughts wouldn't lie still. The crow on the thatch flew into his mind. He'd see to that villain in the morning and put a few pickles in her tail. Some day he'd have the whole house corrugated. Maybe now the kitchen'd be flooded. He was about to get up, when the rain suddenly ceased. It eased his mind, and listening now to the drip-drop of water from the eaves, he slipped into sleep.

But in the morning he didn't get up. His shoulders, arms and legs were stiff and painful. Martha brought him his breakfast, and it was a very subdued man that she saw.

'Give me a lift up, Martha, on the pillows. That's a good girl. Aisy now, aisy!' he said in a slow, pained voice.

'Do you feel bad, Paddy?'

'Bravely, Martha, bravely. There's a wee pain across me shoulder, maybe you'd give it a rub. I'll be all right now when I get a rest.'

'You took too much out of yourself for one day.'

'I know, I know! But it'd take any other man three days to do the same field. Listen, Martha, put the mare out on the side of the hill; a canter round will do her a world of good.'

And so the first day wore on with his limbs aching, Martha coming to attend him, or Kate coming to counsel him. But from his bed he could see the mare clear as a white rock on the face of the hill, and it heartened him to watch her long tail busily swishing. On the bed beside him was his stick and on the floor a battered biscuit tin. Hour after hour he struck the tin with his stick when he wanted something—matches, tobacco, a drink, or his shoulder rubbed. And glad he was if Martha answered his knocking.

Two days passed in this way, and on the morning of

the third the boat with the dealer was due. Time and again Martha went out on a hill at the back of the house, scanning the sea for the boat. At last she saw it and hurried to Kate with the news. Kate made a big bowl of warm punch and brought it to Paddy.

'How do you feel this morning?' she said when she entered the room.

'A lot aisier, thank God, a lot aisier.'

'Take this now and turn in and sleep. It'll do you good.'

Paddy took the warm bowl in his two hands, sipping slowly, and giving an odd cough as the strong whiskey caught his breath. Whenever he paused his eyes were on the window watching the mare on the hillside, and when he had finished, he sighed and lay back happily. His body felt deliciously warm and he smiled sweetly. Poor Kate; he misjudged her; she has a heart of corn and means well. Warm eddies of air flowed slowly through his head, stealing into every corner, filling him with a thoughtless ecstasy, and closing his eyes in sleep.

As he slept the dealer came, and the mare was sold. When he awakened he felt a queer emptiness in the room, as if something had been taken from it. Instinctively he turned to the window and looked out. The mare was nowhere to be seen and the stone-slap had been tumbled. He seized his stick and battered impatiently on the biscuit tin. He was about to get out of bed when Kate came into the room.

'The mare has got out of the field!'

'She has that and what's more she'll never set foot in it again.'

He waited, waited to hear the worst, that she was sick or had broken a leg.

'The dealer was here an hour ago and I sold her, and, let me tell you, I got a good penny for her,' she added a little proudly.

His anger roused him, and he stared at his sister, his eyes fiercely bright and his mouth open. Catching the rail of the bed he raised himself up and glared at her again.

'Lie down, Paddy, like a good man and quieten yourself. Sure we did it for your own good,' she said, trying to make light of it, and fixing the clothes up around his chest. 'What was she but a poor bit of a beast dying with age? And a good bargain we made.'

'Bargain, is it? And me after rearing her since she was a wee foal . . . No; he'll not get her, I tell you! He'll not get her!'

'For the love of God, man, have sense, have reason!'

But he wasn't listening, he threw back the clothes and reached for his trousers. He brushed her aside with his arm, and his hands trembled as he put on his boots. He seized his stick and made for the door. They tried to stop him and he raised his stick to them. 'Don't meddle with me or I'll give you a belt with this!'

He was out, taking the short-cut down by the back of the house, across the hills that led to the quay. He might be in time; they'd hardly have her in the boat yet. Stones in the gaps fell with a crash behind him and he didn't stop to build them up, not caring where sheep strayed or cattle either. His eyes were fixed on the sea, on the mainland where Maggie was going. His heart hammered wildly, hammered with sharp stinging pains, and he had to halt to ease himself.

He thought of his beast, the poor beast that hated noise and fuss, standing nervous on the pier with a rope tied round her four legs. Gradually the rope would tighten, and she would topple with a thud on the uneven stones while the boys around would cheer. It was always a sight for the young, this shipping of beasts in the little sailing boats. The thought maddened him. His breath wheezed and he licked his dry, salty lips.

And soon he came on to the road that swept in a half

circle to the quay. He saw the boat and an oar sticking over the side. He wouldn't have time to go round. Below him jutted a neck of rock near which the boat would pass on her journey out. He might be able to hail them.

He splashed his way through shallow sea-pools on to the rock, scrambled over its mane of wet seaweed, until he reached the furthest point. Sweat was streaming below his hat and he trembled weakly as he saw the black nose of the boat coming towards him. He saw the curling froth below her bow, the bending backs of the men, and heard the wooden thump of the oars. Nearer it came, gathering speed. A large wave tilted the boat and he saw the white side of his mare, lying motionless between the beams. They were opposite him now, a hundred yards from him. He raised his stick and called, but he seemed to have lost his voice. He waved and called again, his voice sounding strange and weak. The man in the stern waved back as he would to a child. The boat passed the rock, leaving a wedge of calm water in her wake. The noise of the oars stopped and the sail filled in the breeze. For a long time he looked at the receding boat, his spirit draining from him. A wave washed up the rock, frothing at his feet, and he turned wearily away, going slowly back the road that led home.